ROYALTY DEFEATED BY LOVE

Bettina had been angry with Michael for kissing her, and yet in her heart she had known that there was something about his kiss that could not make her angry, but made her feel something very different from anger.

It had been so different from that other kiss on the first day. Then he had stolen his pleasure almost casually. She could have been anyone and she had felt insulted.

But the second kiss had been gentle and tender, with a passion and sweetness that she would remember all her life. For a moment she could have sworn that he was thinking of nothing but her.

It was she who had broken the spell by losing her temper, assuming that he was merely making use of her.

But suppose he had not been doing so? Suppose he had really meant it?

She chided herself for her foolishness.

Of course it could come to nothing. Between an Earl and an Army Major's daughter there could never be any thought of marriage.

THE BARBARA CARTLAND PINK COLLECTION

Titles in this series

ROYALTY DEFEATED BY LOVE

BARBARA CARTLAND

Barbaracartland.com Ltd

THE BARBARA CARTLAND PINK COLLECTION

Barbara Cartland was the most prolific bestselling author in the history of the world. She was frequently in the Guinness Book of Records for writing more books in a year than any other living author. In fact her most amazing literary feat was when her publishers asked for more Barbara Cartland romances, she doubled her output from 10 books a year to over 20 books a year, when she was 77.

She went on writing continuously at this rate for 20 years and wrote her last book at the age of 97, thus completing 400 books between the ages of 77 and 97.

Her publishers finally could not keep up with this phenomenal output, so at her death she left 160 unpublished manuscripts, something again that no other author has ever achieved.

Now the exciting news is that these 160 original unpublished Barbara Cartland books are ready for publication and they will be published by Barbaracartland.com exclusively on the internet, as the web is the best possible way to reach so many Barbara Cartland readers around the world.

The 160 books will be published monthly and will be numbered in sequence.

The series is called the Pink Collection as a tribute to Barbara Cartland whose favourite colour was pink and it became very much her trademark over the years.

The Barbara Cartland Pink Collection is published only on the internet. Log on to www.barbaracartland.com to find out how you can purchase the books monthly as they are published, and take out a subscription that will ensure that all subsequent editions are delivered to you by mail order to your home.

If you do not have access to a computer you can write for information about the Pink Collection to the following address :

Barbara Cartland.com Ltd.
Camfield Place,
Hatfield,
Hertfordshire AL9 6JE
United Kingdom.

Telephone :   +44 (0)1707 642629
Fax :   +44 (0)1707 663041

THE LATE DAME BARBARA CARTLAND

Barbara Cartland who sadly died in May 2000 at the age of nearly 99 was the world's most famous romantic novelist who wrote 723 books in her lifetime with worldwide sales of over 1 billion copies and her books were translated into 36 different languages.

As well as romantic novels, she wrote historical biographies, 6 autobiographies, theatrical plays, books of advice on life, love, vitamins and cookery. She also found time to be a political speaker and television and radio personality.

She wrote her first book at the age of 21 and this was called *Jigsaw*. It became an immediate bestseller and sold 100,000 copies in hardback and was translated into 6 different languages. She wrote continuously throughout her life, writing bestsellers for an astonishing 76 years. Her books have always been immensely popular in the United States, where in 1976 her current books were at numbers 1 & 2 in the B. Dalton bestsellers list, a feat never achieved before or since by any author.

Barbara Cartland became a legend in her own lifetime and will be best remembered for her wonderful romantic novels, so loved by her millions of readers throughout the world.

Her books will always be treasured for their moral message, her pure and innocent heroines, her good looking and dashing heroes and above all her belief that the power of love is more important than anything else in everyone's life.

"Love, love, love, is all that matters in this world and the next."

Barbara Cartland

CHAPTER ONE
1878

As the hansom cab turned the corner into Belgrave Square, Lord Winton Shriver said,

"You are looking very down-in-the-mouth, old fellow. If I had your life I think I would be fairly cheerful."

Michael, Earl of Danesbury, gave his friend a rueful grin.

"If you had my life, Win, you would run a mile. You know what is going to happen when we reach this party, don't you?"

"Yes, we are going to celebrate the engagement of our old friend, Viscount Allerton, to the Honourable Laura Conway. Mind you, just the thought of it depresses me."

Lord Winton's handsome, willowy person, seemed to shrink into the corner of the cab at the mere idea of marriage.

Lord Danesbury, equally handsome but more robustly built, grinned at his friend. Winton, 'Win' to his friends, was a flirt – a hardened flirt some said, although it had always seemed to Michael Danesbury that it was his soft-heartedness that got him into trouble.

Win simply could not see a pretty face without going weak at the knees. But he fled all suggestions of marriage like the plague.

Michael also avoided marriage but for different reasons. Since he had become Earl of Danesbury three years ago, he had been a target for matchmaking Mamas and their eager daughters.

He wanted none of them. But he knew that tonight, as always, he would have to dodge the webs that were being spun for him.

Now he repeated his question.

"You know what will happen when we arrive at Conway House, don't you?"

"You will be surrounded by beautiful girls, all trying to catch your attention," Win observed. "Don't ask me to feel sorry for you!"

"Well you should. Beautiful they may be, but each one of them has the light of matrimony in her eyes. They do not see me, they see my coronet. They see being Mistress of Danesbury House and Danesbury Castle."

"So take your pick of them."

"No, that is not good enough for me. I want a woman who loves me for myself alone, without caring about the title."

"But how will you ever know?" Win pointed out practically.

"I shall know. When I meet the one and only, I shall know that her heart is true and honest. Otherwise, she is not the one for me."

"Well, you be careful," Win warned. "Some of the parents are getting very clever. Do you know how James Allerton came to propose to Laura?"

"I have heard some disquieting rumours."

"The truth is that he never did propose to her. Her father asked to see the Queen and said he had damaged her reputation, just because they talked for too long in the garden."

"So the rumours *are* true!" Michael exclaimed with a touch of alarm.

"Her Majesty sent for Allerton and told him she would not tolerate 'such behaviour'. The Prince of Wales was there and he said he could not abide any scandal."

"Him?" Michael echoed in disgust. "The man is a walking scandal himself! One mistress after another. Only recently he was threatened with blackmail on account of some letters he had written to one of them."

"That is why he is being a bit careful at the moment. He told Allerton that he could only associate with 'men of good character', so he must either 'do the decent thing' or be dismissed from HRH's circle."

"Damned hypocrite!" Michael observed.

"I could not agree more, old boy. But that is how it's done these days and you can be sure that the Randalls know it. You had better watch out."

"I don't know what you mean," Michael replied uncomfortably.

"Oh, yes, you do. Lady Alice has been trying to get her pretty little claws into you for some time."

"Well, she hasn't succeeded."

"My point exactly. She is becoming frustrated. So are her parents. And frustration breeds ideas."

"Dammit Win, I've a good mind to jump out of this cab and run for it."

"Too late. You have formally accepted the invitation, and we're nearly there."

Michael groaned, but it was true. The hansom cab was drawing up in front of a house which was brilliantly lit in every window.

From inside came the sound of music and the large front door was open as a stream of gorgeously dressed guests

3

entered, to be received by a punctilious butler.

Their hosts greeted them with delight. Michael responded with the right words, but he was already looking around apprehensively for the Randall family.

And as soon as he entered the ballroom he noticed Lady Alice Randall. She immediately ran towards him and put her hand on his arm.

"I am so glad you have come," she gushed. "All the other men are so boring. I was just so hoping you would be here and we could dance together."

"Of course we can," Michael agreed politely.

He saw her eyes turned up to him.

He thought they were dangerous. They told him, without any words, what she wanted.

The next moment she had slipped her hand into his.

He knew the gesture would not go unnoticed by a great number of guests present who were the worst gossips in the whole of Mayfair.

"You are so late," she sighed. "I thought you had forgotten about me."

"Of course I had not forgotten you," he replied, knowing it was expected of him.

He was in fact wondering how he could prevent her from holding so tightly on to his arm and moving closer and closer to him.

She was very pretty but was not exactly a *debutante* as she had been out in Society for two years. But he recognised that she had set her cap at him and it was impossible for him to avoid her.

She turned up at every party he attended. She always had something to tell him which would mean her holding on to his arm and talking to him in a way which made it difficult for him to move away.

He had hoped that tonight she would not be so clinging, as the focus of attention should be on the engaged couple.

It was, however, quite obvious that Alice had no intention of leaving him.

"Do come and see James and Laura," she urged. "They are so happy. Isn't it the most delightful thing in the world to see a happy engaged couple?"

His mouth felt dry.

"Delightful," he muttered.

As they walked down the room, Michael was aware that a great number of eyes would be watching them. The chaperones wanted to know if, after so many trials which had failed, his heart had been captured by Alice.

When they reached the 'happy couple' Michael recognised that his worst fears had been realised. Viscount Allerton looked like a turkey trussed for the slaughter. His bride, who normally looked belligerent and ill-natured, now looked belligerent and triumphant.

He paid the necessary compliments, assured Viscout Allerton that he was the luckiest man alive and received a ghastly smile in return.

Then there was a tug on Michael's arm and he realised that Alice was still standing there.

He had almost forgotten her existence.

But now he felt annoyed that she was more or less forcing herself upon him, and behaving as if he belonged to her and owed her his entire attention.

He forced a smile to his face. He had an uncomfortable feeling that it must mirror Viscount Allerton's.

The music was playing. Firmly Alice pulled him away.

5

"I want to dance with you," she said. "I have been waiting for too long."

"There are plenty of other men with whom you could dance," Michael suggested hopefully.

"But I only want you," Alice whispered. "You dance so divinely and are so different from anyone else. When I am in your arms I feel as if we are dancing up into the sky amongst the stars."

There was a note in her voice which made Michael stiffen.

"How nice," he said lamely, inwardly praying for something to save him.

Against all the odds, something did happen. There was a little commotion in the crowd. The musicians fell silent. The dancers moved aside to make a space as a voice from the door boomed,

"His Royal Highness, the Prince of Wales."

The next moment a very large man appeared. He was in his late thirties, with a fleshy, self-indulgent face, only partly hidden by a beard. More self-indulgence showed in his girth and his hair was growing thin.

But he possessed an imposing dignity that nothing could take away. He was the heir to the throne of England.

He advanced slowly the length of the ballroom, receiving the curtsies of the ladies and bows from the gentlemen.

When he reached the engaged couple his smile was affable. Whatever arms he had had to twist to bring about their engagement, he was in a good mood now and determined to enjoy himself.

"Allerton, you lucky dog!" he boomed. "I wish you every happiness, I do indeed."

"As Your Royal Highness pleases," Viscount Allerton recited mechanically, with a little bow.

"Not as *I* please," the Prince of Wales corrected him. "This betrothal is *your* pleasure and now I have met the lady, I understand why.

"Laura, my dear, if you knew how often he has sighed over you, thinking he had no hope, until at last I told him to take courage and risk a declaration. 'Mark my words, Allerton,' I said, 'the lady will not be hard on you.' And I was right, was I not?"

Laura gave a simpering giggle, guaranteed to set any man's teeth on edge. Even her giggle managed to be belligerent, Michael noticed.

"So you see," the Prince continued mercilessly, "I take the credit for this engagement. I brought about the whole betrothal."

Everyone applauded. Under cover of the noise, Win muttered in Michael's ear,

"That much is certainly true."

The orchestra struck up again. The Prince took the floor with Laura. He danced well and elegantly for so heavy a man.

In fact, he possessed all the social skills, except the ability to be faithful to his wife. On a recent trip to India he had fought off Princess Alexandra's attempts to accompany him for reasons that were the talk of London. Needless to say, the Princess was not with him tonight.

And this was the man who had forced Viscount Allerton to become engaged to a girl he did not love, because he could only be associated with 'men of good character'.

Michael looked around quickly before Alice could claim him again and found himself another partner. The blissful maiden sank into his arms, dreaming of a coronet.

He danced with her only once nor did she expect more. He was becoming too worried to risk a second dance with anyone. Everyone knew that Lord Danesbury was Alice's –

if she could catch him.

When the music stopped, Michael was saved from Alice by the Prince himself who demanded that he join him for a brandy in the smoking room with their host and some other gentlemen.

But even here there was no escape. The Prince was in teasing mood.

"One wedding begets another, eh, Danesbury?"

"We cannot all be as lucky as Allerton, Your Royal Highness. By the way, may I congratulate you on the success of your horses at Ascot?"

This was a clear breach of protocol, since only Royalty were allowed to change the subject. Luckily the Prince was always ready to discuss his horses and the dangerous moment passed.

Michael breathed a sigh of relief when the Prince departed, but almost at once he felt Alice's hand on his arm again.

"Shall we have a little fresh air?" she suggested.

Resigning himself to his fate, he allowed her to lead him towards the French windows which led into the garden, where there were drinks and plenty of food for everyone to enjoy.

The trees had been decorated with fairy lights.

It would all have been charming, if he had not been so acutely alert for danger.

He was well aware that if they moved into the shadows of the trees, she would want him to kiss her.

'She is a damn nuisance,' he thought to himself. 'But how can I get rid of her?'

It was impossible for him to do so.

Against his will, Michael found himself drawn under the glittering trees and into the darkness beyond them.

The soft light in that part of the garden came only from the moon and stars above.

"At last we are alone," Alice breathed softly.

"I have brought you here because I want to tell you how wonderful you are and how much I love being with you."

"And I enjoy being with you," he responded untruthfully, "but I have no wish to be rude to my hostess."

He would have moved away as he spoke, but Alice stood in front of him.

"I want you to stay with me," she said. "I love you, I love you, and when I told Papa that we were so happy together, he was delighted. He said you were just the son-in-law he always wanted."

Michael was too shocked to speak.

Son-in-law?

Taking advantage of his stillness, Alice slipped her arms about his neck.

"You don't have to hide your feelings while we are alone," she whispered, pulling his head down.

His lips were against hers.

'If anyone should see us now,' he thought wildly.

He tried to disengage himself without being brutal, but her arms were like ropes about him.

And then there was a loud yell from somewhere in the darkness.

"Good Heavens, what's that?" he cried, managing to release himself at last.

"What does it matter?" Alice asked.

"It sounds like some creature in pain," he said. "We must render assistance."

"Someone else will do that," Alice replied, growing

petulant as she sensed her victory being snatched from her.

"My dear girl, we really must – Winton, whatever has happened?"

"I fell over some dashed tree root," Win said, limping out of the shadows. "Took a nasty tumble."

His person was as immaculate as ever and he did not look like a man who had taken a tumble, but Michael was all solicitude, giving Win his arm.

"Let's get you back to the house," he offered.

Alice glared.

It was wonderful how Win's limp became more pronounced when they reached the house. He threw in the odd groan for effect, enabling Michael to say to his hosts,

"I should take my friend home as soon as possible. If a cab could be summoned – "

A footman hurried to the cab rank just around the corner and within a few minutes the two men were making their escape.

Michael hurried away without meeting Alice's eyes.

*

"I am deeply in your debt, Win."

It was two hours later and they were deep in the heart of the Davenham Club. Having played cards and sustained heavy losses, they were now engaged in drinking brandy.

"Well I had to do something, old fellow," Win said. "From where I was standing I could see that you were in a bad way. Desperate measures were needed."

Michael grinned.

"You certainly saved the day. The way you were yowling I thought there really was something wrong with you."

"But what are you going to do next time?" Win wanted to know.

"I cannot afford a next time. I will have to leave London."

"Where will you go?"

"Perhaps it is time I went to see my castle."

Win stared. When Michael spoke of the castle he meant the ancient home of the Danesburys that had fallen into such a state of disrepair that no Danesbury now wanted to live in it.

"I suppose I should have shown some interest in the place before now," Michael admitted ruefully, "but I never expected to succeed to the title. When my uncle died three years ago, he was still young enough to marry and beget an heir.

"And then suddenly he was gone and I became the Earl. Since then I suppose I have not paid enough attention to my responsibilities, chiefly because I have been concentrating on making money."

Michael's father had left him only a modest fortune and the money he had inherited from his uncle was barely adequate.

But he possessed brains and good contacts. He had taken some of his inheritance, borrowed from the bank, and invested in the railways that were fast covering the country.

Now he was a very rich man indeed.

"I could afford to put that place in order," he mused. "So I suppose it *is* my duty to do so. It is what all my relatives have been telling me for the last three years."

"This sudden interest in your duty would not have anything to do with Alice Randall, would it?" Win enquired cynically.

Michael grinned.

"I suppose it might. Dash it all, Win, do women ever think of anything else but marriage?"

"You are an Earl, my dear boy. You are twenty-seven and good-looking, so my sisters assure me. And you are intelligent."

"How would you know?" Michael demanded. Win was more famous for his charm and good nature than the sharpness of his wits.

He acknowledged this dart with his usual amiability.

"True, I confess it. But you are more intelligent than me. That much I can be certain about. You are also wealthy and unattached. What else but marriage do you expect them to think about?"

"Do they never think of love?" Michael asked.

Win laughed.

"Love looks its best when it has a tiara glittering on its head and diamonds around its neck!"

"So they all seem to think. Well, I am off for a spell in the country. If the castle is as bad as they say, at least it will act as a form of protection from determined females."

"Where exactly is this place?"

"About forty miles South of London, near a little village called Hedgeworth. I think I will leave tomorrow."

Win shifted uncomfortably.

"Actually, old boy, you wouldn't like some company, would you?"

"If you mean yourself, I would be delighted. But Win, have you thought? I gather the place is in very poor repair. We will be living rough. You are a gentleman of London Society. You are only at ease amid elegance and comfort."

"Elegance and comfort take money, old boy, and I have none. I lost a pile in the last hour and the Pater isn't going to be pleased. I thought I might put off that meeting by throwing myself on your mercy."

"Of course. As I said, I am in your debt. I will be glad

to help you in any way I can. But when we reach the castle and you find yourself living in a pigsty, don't say I did not warn you."

"You have my word on it," Win replied.

As they left the club he asked anxiously,

"You don't actually mean a pigsty, do you?"

Michael's chuckle floated back on the wind.

*

"Papa! Papa, are you there?"

Bettina Newton paused in the garden of her home in the heart of Hedgeworth village, looking round for her father. Everywhere she turned she saw herbs and flowers in full bloom and she delayed for a moment to enjoy them.

She was like a flower herself, twenty years old, with fair golden hair and glowing skin. Her eyes were an incredibly deep blue.

She wondered if her father was in the garden, tending to his herbs. She needed to see him because she had been to visit a sick woman in the village and she wanted his advice.

Even after working with him for a year or so, she was still uncertain of what to do when someone had contracted an unfamiliar disease.

She often thought it strange that a soldier, which her father had been until he retired, should know so much about curing the sick.

But before he was in the Army and afterwards, he had loved gardens and everything which grew naturally.

After he had served in India and elsewhere in the East, he had grown to know even more about flowers and herbs.

He had learnt the way they should be made to grow so that they were not only beautiful to the eye, but also helpful in a great number of ways to the body.

When he left the Army he had retired to Hedgeworth, where he had lived many years ago and of which he maintained very fond memories. For the last four years he and Bettina had lived here very happily and his reputation had grown, sometimes to the annoyance of the local medical profession.

Bettina had often thought it extraordinary that the ordinary physicians, especially those who only attended country people, knew so little about the natural remedies which were to be found in flowers and herbs.

It seemed to her that these benefits came from God, while what the doctors provided came only from men and were not natural or what the body really needed.

She hurried into the house, through the hall and down the passage and finally found her father in the library, where he had his desk.

As she opened the door he raised his head and said,

"You are back, my darling, rather sooner than I expected."

"I need something for Mrs. Brown," she replied. "She is coughing so badly and the medicine the doctor gave her has had no effect."

The Major gave a sigh as he rose from his desk.

"I was just designing a new path so that we can reach the river from our garden," he said. "I am sure that when you see the plan you will think it is as pretty as I intend it to be."

"Dearest Papa, I know you would much rather be working on your new garden, but I am really worried about Mrs. Brown."

"You worry yourself about too many people," her father said. "Before we came to live here the village was quite content with the doctor, if he would condescend to come to them."

"But they have *you* now."

"Yes and I believe they send for me because they think I am more interesting and certainly more amusing than Dr. Smythe."

Bettina laughed.

"That would not be difficult," she said. "He is so gloomy that I am sure he makes people feel worse as soon as they see him. They much prefer you."

"Yes, and it makes Dr. Smythe furious," he responded wryly.

Because he was so successful the Major found it impossible to refuse to do what he could for the people who asked for help.

But it frustrated him, because it prevented him from working on his garden, which he loved and adored.

He was, in fact, preparing to write a book as his daughter had insisted he should do.

In it he would show not only how to arrange a garden to make it beautiful, but also to make sure it contained healing herbs.

If people praised him he would say,

"You forget how much I have travelled. Since I was in the Army I was lucky enough, at Her Majesty's expense, to have seen a great deal of the world. I have learnt from those countries, especially in the East, that the Almighty, not mankind, has provided a cure for almost every human illness."

Bettina knew that he had chosen to return to this house because of its large unkempt garden that he could transform.

And yet she realised that part of him wanted to be on the move again. He was too clever a man to be shut away in this backward place. He needed to be exploring the world, in search of new plants.

It was only the lack of money that kept him here.

'Then perhaps I should be glad that we are short of money,' she said to herself. 'I will try to be glad but – I would not mind just a *little* more."

The Major was a gentleman and he lived like one, but in a very modest way. He had a tiny private income and a small Army pension. Their life was reasonably comfortable, but every comfort was achieved by clever management.

The house was the largest in the village and they needed the room for all the Major's books and botanical specimens.

A middle-aged couple lived at the back. Mrs. Gates was the cook and Mr. Gates worked in the garden, but only under the Major's strict supervision. It was his constant complaint that he was not allowed to prune and tend as he wished, but must follow his Master's strict rules.

In addition he drove the shabby gig that they kept for very special occasions. These included dinner with the Mayor or the Lord Lieutenant, for, despite his straightened circumstances, Major Newton was known as a man of learning and cultivation.

The addition of a scullery maid completed the roster of servants. If there was any domestic work left over to do, Bettina would roll up her sleeves and do it herself.

She did it willingly, but she longed for some small luxuries, like good clothes. She made herself a new dress once a year and while she made it well, she would have much preferred to be able to afford a proper seamstress and a touch of fashion.

The deep blue dress she commonly wore was good enough in its way, but she often covered it with a large white apron. If the weather was hot and she was working in the garden, she covered her hair with a white cotton sun bonnet.

In short, she frequently looked like a servant. Of

course, it did not matter in the village, where everyone knew that she was a lady. But sometimes it depressed her a little.

She wandered out into the garden again to collect some mint to be used in the cooking of her father's dinner.

As she strolled amid the blooms, she gazed up at the great building that filled the view.

Everyone knew that the castle belonged to the Earl of Danesbury, but nobody seemed to know any more than that.

The Earl had never been to see it and nobody in the village even knew what he looked like.

'If only he were to come here,' she thought wistfully. 'He could make the whole area more prosperous. And it would be lovely to have just a little excitement.'

Then she remembered her school days and how the other girls had looked down on her because their fathers boasted titles and hers did not.

'Oh, what difference would it make?' she sighed to herself. 'If, by some miracle the Earl did come to live here, I am the very last person who would ever be asked to meet him.'

CHAPTER TWO

For a journey of only forty miles Michael decided to use his own post-chaise rather than take the train.

On leaving the club he and Win travelled straight to Win's rooms and instructed his valet to start packing his clothes for departure in the morning.

"And prepare for a siege, Joshua," Win said in a voice of doom. "We are going into unknown territory. His Lordship describes the place in the darkest terms."

"A pigsty," Michael confirmed, grinning.

Joshua blenched, but did not flinch.

"There is still a skeleton staff at the castle," Michael said, "but that is all I know. There will not be much in the way of creature comforts."

Joshua stood to attention.

"I am prepared, my Lord."

"Stout fellow!" Win exclaimed emotionally.

Grinning, Michael left them.

Leroy, his own valet was equally stoical about the horrors in store for him and by the time they were ready to leave, he had packed up almost all the clothes Michael possessed.

"We're going into the country, my Lord," he declared in the voice of one facing execution. "And it will be necessary to maintain standards."

Michael did not contradict him, but he was privately looking forward to dressing more quietly than he could in London.

When the morning came he scandalised his faithful henchman by insisting on wearing his plainest suit and a hat that made Leroy blench.

The hat was called a '*wideawake*' and was a low-crowned, wide-brimmed creation made of felt that looked, Leroy thought, like an upturned breakfast cup on a very large saucer.

It was decidedly informal, made for country wear, preferably by the lower orders. Michael had started to wear one during his extensive travels, before he had inherited his title. Now he refused to part with it.

This morning he perched it defiantly on his head.

Nobody, thought Leroy in horror, would have guessed that this was one of the finest sprigs of the British aristocracy. But he made no comment, knowing that, behind an amiable temper, Lord Danesbury hid an awesome obstinacy.

Before leaving, Michael spoke to his butler.

"If anyone asks for me, you are to say that I have gone to the country. You are not certain where, but you think it's somewhere in the North of England."

"I understand your Lordship does not wish to be followed."

"Exactly. And make sure that no one in the house answers any questions put to them."

Finally he had a word with his secretary, instructing him to cancel all his invitations.

"And I do employ a skeleton staff, don't I? It occurs to be that I might have imagined it and will arrive to find the place totally deserted."

"Your Lordship pays the wages of a Mr. and Mrs. Brooks, just to ensure that the place isn't left completely empty," replied the secretary.

Arriving at Win's rooms, he found that his friend had taken exactly the opposite sartorial direction to himself and was dressed with extreme finery, as though in defiance of Fate. His frock coat was elegant and his top hat was perfection.

"Good grief, Danesbury!" he exclaimed, on seeing Michael's attire. *"What on earth is that thing on your head?"*

"It's my *wideawake*. Have you never seen one before?"

"Thankfully no and I shall endeavour to avert my eyes so that I do not have to see it again. You don't seriously expect me to be seen with you dressed like that? People will think you are my man."

"Nonsense, Win. You dress your man far better than this!"

Laughing, they climbed into the post-chaise, while their valets followed behind in a fourgon with all the luggage.

It was a brilliant summer's day and the two young men were in high spirits as they left London behind, both in their different ways fleeing trouble.

For lunch they stopped at a country inn and ate outside, enjoying the sunshine and the feeling of freedom. One or two people gave them odd looks.

"It's the way you are dressed," Win muttered. "I told you, everyone will think you are a servant and they wonder why we are eating at the same table."

"Yes, my Lord." Michael grinned

'How good it feels to eat country food and drink country ale,' he thought. They climbed back into the chaise and spent the next couple of hours watching the scenery stream by.

At last they gained their first glimpse of the castle, silhouetted against the sky with the garden around it and the trees beyond.

It seemed to Michael that it exuded a charm which he had never noticed before.

"Is that your castle?" Win asked.

"That is indeed my castle," Michael said, feeling a certain pride as he pronounced *"my* castle".

"It is very beautiful," Win said.

"Yes, it is. Let us stop for a moment."

Michael called to the coachman to stop and they climbed down to survey the countryside.

They were close to a village which, he guessed, must be Hedgeworth. It was a tiny hamlet with one main high street ending in a stone house, set in a large garden filled with flowers.

All around them the scenery was gentle and beautiful, the trees in bloom and the flowers glowing with a hundred pretty colours.

Now he was glad of his unobtrusive clothing. Win's sartorial glory looked rather out of place in these surroundings.

Suddenly floating on the bright air came wafting the sound of a young girl's voice singing.

"Where the sweet river wanders,
My love and I walked,
He smiled and said 'Dearest,
Come talk with me, talk.

Let's speak of the future
That shines bright before us,
And never, never be parted again'."

Michael stood quite still, entranced by the purity of the girl's voice.

He could not see anybody, but the sound seemed to be coming from his left, where there was a small river, with weeping willows hanging down to the water and reeds breaking the surface. He thought he had never witnessed anything so charming.

The next moment he realised that there was something else in the world that was even more charming. As he moved forward he saw a girl in a deep blue dress, kneeling on the bank, gathering reeds.

He could not see her face clearly, but what little he could see was pretty and country fresh with soft cheeks like peaches and cream.

Her figure was slim and elegant and beneath her white, cotton sun bonnet he could just spy a glimpse of golden hair.

Then she began to sing again.

"*Never be parted,*
Aye those were his words.
But oh, life is cruel,
And now he has gone.
The river still wanders,
But I walk alone."

The soft melancholy of the last words died away, and the girl continued with her work, oblivious to the onlooker standing there or how she had affected him.

Michael contemplated her, thinking how sweet and natural she looked. In fact, she was the most delightful sight he had seen for a very long time.

He smiled with pleasure.

He was going to enjoy the country life.

At that moment the girl leaned forward to reach a distant reed, but it was a little too far. She tried again, stretching further.

"Hey!" Michael called.

He could see she had leaned at too great an angle and was heading for a fall. Running fast, he just managed to reach her in time and seize her about the waist.

"It's all right," he cried. "I've caught you."

"Oh – thank you," she gasped.

He moved a step back, taking her with him and lifting her, so that she was drawn to her feet. She seized his arms, steadying herself and catching her breath.

But at the last minute Michael lost his balance and fell backwards, taking her to the ground with him in an undignified sprawl that dislodged her bonnet.

All her shining fair hair came tumbling down around her shoulders, in a seemingly endless golden stream. Down and down it coursed, almost to her waist, gleaming in the sun.

She burst out laughing and it seemed to Michael's enchanted senses that her laughter was one with the gold of her hair. Like music it rippled and shivered away into the glowing sunlit air.

"Thank you so much," she said recovering her poise. "I so nearly fell into the water."

"That would have been terrible," Michael agreed. "I am so glad I managed to save you, but sorry I was so clumsy about it."

"Oh, that doesn't matter," she said cheerfully. "I have lived in the country long enough not to worry about a tumble now and then."

After the self-conscious frailty of the elegant ladies that he met in London, this was music to Michael's ears.

He helped her to pick up the reeds which had become strewn everywhere and placed them neatly into her basket.

He caught her looking at him curiously.

"You are a stranger here?" she asked.

"That's right."

"In this tiny place a new face always stands out. If you are looking for an inn, there's – "

"No, thank you," he interrupted her, laughing. "We don't need an inn. We are staying at the castle."

"We?"

She looked around and her eyes lit on Win, strolling some distance away, in all his magnificence. Her jaw dropped.

"You don't mean – ? Lord Danesbury has returned to the castle at last?"

"That's right."

"But how wonderful! It will mean so much to the village – to everyone around here. It seemed so sad that he never thought of us. Will he stay long, do you think?"

"Well, I – "

"It will mean jobs, for he will want to hire people. Oh, this is such good news!"

"Has the castle been empty for very long?" he asked cautiously.

"Oh, *years*. At least – it isn't precisely empty. There's Brooks and his wife. He used to be the butler, but he is really more of a caretaker now. I believe the place is in a shocking state. Lord Danesbury really ought to be ashamed of himself!"

She glared in the direction of Win's beautiful person. He was standing looking at the castle through an extremely

24

elegant gold eyeglass. Michael had always stigmatised this piece of adornment as dandified, but there was no doubt that it made its owner look impressive.

"Look at him," she said as the sun winked off the eyeglass. "I'll wager that object he is holding up to his eye is solid gold."

"It is," Michael confirmed, his eyes dancing.

"Well, that just tells you, doesn't it?"

"Tells me what?"

"That he is a man who spends his money on personal decoration and thinks nothing of his responsibilities. The castle needs money spent on it and so does the district. And what does he use his money for? A gold eyeglass."

Michael recognised that he should speak up at once, but an imp of mischief teased him to continue such an innocent deception a little further.

"He is not entirely to blame," he ventured, keeping a straight face. "He never expected to inherit the title. He always thought his uncle would marry and produce a son and heir but then the uncle died suddenly."

"How long ago was that?"

"Three years," he admitted.

"Three years when he did not even bother to visit his ancestral home? I call that shocking."

"You may be right," he conceded meekly. "I don't think he ever saw the matter in that light."

It occurred to him that for a servant girl she boasted an unusually educated accent. She might almost have been a lady. But no lady dressed like this and plucked reeds from the river.

Michael wondered if she was one of his tenants and thought that she probably must be. His land stretched for a long way around the castle.

"Tell me, is this what you normally do?"

"Gathering reeds? No, I usually work in the garden."

"What is your name?" he asked, smiling. "No, don't tell me, let me guess. Rose, or Lily, Lilac, Iris or perhaps Hyacinth. I feel sure that you are named after some beautiful flower."

Bettina regarded him wryly.

"Indeed!" she said. "Perhaps you should be careful, lest I turn out to be called Stinging Nettle."

"I don't believe it. Such a pretty miss must be quite without venom."

"Do you always talk to strange girls in this manner."

"Only if they are devastatingly beautiful. If you are not named after a flower then you must be something else that is lovely, such as Faith, Hope or Charity."

She gave a choke of laughter and quickly placed her hand over her mouth.

"I am sorry," she said. "But you are being so absurd."

"I was trying to make myself agreeable," he protested.

"To whom? There may be some females who find it agreeable to listen to condescending nonsense. I am not one of them."

"I am sure I don't know what you mean by 'condescending'."

"I think you do. You come from London, full of your own importance. You see me gathering reeds and you think, 'Hah!'"

"I never said 'Hah!" he defended himself.

"You thought it. 'Hah! A raw country girl, a silly creature who knows no better. She will be flattered at my even talking to her. A few idiotic remarks about roses and lilacs and she will melt.' Well sir, do I look as though I am melting?"

"Most certainly you do not," Michael answered, trying to keep a clear head.

It was like being attacked by a swarm of bees, he thought.

At the same time, she was enchanting. The more she flew at him in a whirlwind of indignation, the more enchanting she became.

His senses grew dizzy. His mind was swimming with the thoughts and sensations that were surging through him. As she grew angry the colour had mounted in her cheeks until he thought he had never seen anyone so lovely.

Suddenly Michael could not resist any longer. Nor, to be honest, did he try very hard.

Fixing his eyes on her adorable face, he pulled her forward and placed a kiss firmly on her red lips.

At first she did not move. He could feel her go tense with shock and waited for her to soften, sharing his pleasure. Not for one instant did he doubt that, despite her pretty indignation, she was secretly willing.

For a long moment he enjoyed the sensation of her beautiful mouth against his, so soft and – as he convinced himself – yielding.

But then his illusion was shattered. With one firm movement the girl freed herself from him. Taken aback, he stared at her.

The next moment he was reeling from a slap on the face that almost made him see stars.

"Hey!" he exclaimed.

"How dare you!" she breathed. "What do you think I – ? Who do you – ? *How dare you!*"

"I am sorry," he said hastily. "I beg your pardon. Perhaps that was unwise of me but – "

"*Unwise?* Is that all you can say? I could think of a

much worse word. Disgraceful. Not the action of a gentleman with any decency or honour."

"Was I really to blame?" he pleaded, half humorously. "What *can* I do when you look so pretty?"

"Are you daring to suggest that it was my fault?"

"I cannot be the first man who has wanted to kiss you?"

"As to that, I would not know, but you are certainly the first who has forgotten his manners enough to do so," she raged.

"Don't you think you are making too much of it?" he declared. "After all, it was only one little kiss."

She drew herself up and gave him a fierce look.

"I am betrothed," she announced in a withering voice.

He froze, appalled.

Somehow it had never occurred to Michael that this might be so. She had seemed to be so natural, so much a part of the summer day, like a gift from Heaven. Now he discovered that he might have compromised her.

Looking round, he saw to his relief that they were unobserved.

"I beg your pardon," he muttered. "Obviously I should not have – please excuse me."

He hurried away without another word, wondering what had come over him to behave in such a way.

But he had not been able to stop himself. That was the truth.

"Drive on," he told the coachman as he and Win climbed back into the carriage.

"Did you have an accident?" Win asked, regarding him sympathetically.

"No, why?"

"Your face is red on one side. I wondered if you had suffered a fall."

"I stumbled and – er – fell against a tree," Michael said, rubbing his face self-consciously.

"A tree? Surely there were no trees in the direction you – ?"

"For the love of Heaven, Win!" he roared. "Let the matter rest!"

"All right, all right. No need to get in a miff."

*

The castle was beautiful from any angle, but as they drove up to the front door, Michael could see that the windows needed replacing and the doors required repainting.

Stepping out of the chaise, he said to the coachman,

"You can find your way to the stables, although I doubt if there will be anyone there."

The way he spoke made his coachman laugh.

"This be a real adventure, my Lord," he said. "I only 'opes you'll not be disappointed."

"We will have to make sure we are not," Michael replied. "Ready for an adventure, Win?"

"Game for anything, old boy!"

Together they walked in through the front door, which Michael was not surprised to find unlocked.

In fact the lock was broken. However there were bolts attached to it, which enabled it to be fastened at night.

The hall was dusty and in need of cleaning. But on the walls hung pictures of his ancestors which he guessed were valuable.

The hall divided into two long corridors, each of which contained furniture that also struck him as valuable.

"I say, suppose there is nobody here at all," Win remarked.

"That girl said there was a caretaker, if we could find him."

"Girl?"

"Er – a local maiden that I chatted with," Michael explained quickly.

He took the left-hand corridor, heading to what he believed was the kitchen.

He had barely reached it when a door opened and an elderly man emerged. He was very untidily dressed and wore no collar.

He glared at Michael and barked,

"Who are you and what do you want?"

"I am Lord Danesbury," Michael said. "I should have told you I was arriving here, but I left London rather unexpectedly."

The man stared at him.

Then he said,

"You be his Lordship, the Earl?"

Michael nodded.

There was silence for a moment, while the man stared at him.

"You could knock me down with a feather, my Lord. I never expected you to come like this. I hoped you would be here sooner or later to see what was happening, but when time passed, and you didn't come, I thought you had forgotten us."

"That was wrong of me," Michael admitted, with his charming smile. "I have sadly neglected my duty. But I am here now. I think you must be Brooks."

The elderly man drew in his breath.

"That's right, my Lord," he said. "I've been here nigh on forty years. I came here first when I was a boy and my mother worked in the kitchen. Then as I grew older I became a footman, as you might call it, and later the butler."

"That is excellent," Michael said. "There is so much I want to know about this castle and you will be able to tell me all."

The door opened again and an elderly woman appeared, giving a little shriek when she saw Michael.

"You must be Mrs. Brooks," he said, giving her too a smile that won her over. "I am Lord Danesbury. It is unpardonable of me to descend on you without warning, but perhaps this will make it a little easier."

He produced some guineas from his pocket and dropped them into her hand.

"There should be enough there to purchase supplies to feed us tonight," he said. "And tomorrow I will provide you with some proper housekeeping money."

"Thank you, my Lord," she said humbly.

"This is my friend, Lord Winton Shriver. He and I will need two rooms, which our valets will make ready, if you have any that are habitable."

"There's the Master's room and the best guest room," Brooks said. "I only hopes that your Lordships will not find them too uncomfortable."

Win's face expressed the same hope.

Luck favoured him. The two rooms, although shabby, were in good condition and their respective valets soon made them comfortable.

When both young men had dressed for dinner, Michael presented himself at Win's door, ready to escort him downstairs.

"This is going to be a voyage of exploration," he said.

"I do not know anything about this place. I was twelve when I saw it last.

"My uncle descended on me one day and said it was time I visited the ancestral home. I did not want to. My uncle scared me because he always expected me to be cleverer than I was, but by mother insisted."

"And you don't recall anything about it?"

"Only that I felt very disappointed because it was so dilapidated. The windows were covered in creepers. The drive had not been cleared of weeds for a long time.

"It was certainly not my idea of an ancestral home. As I toured round with my uncle, I saw so much that was wrong that I kept very quiet. I did not dare tell him what I really thought. He didn't say much either. He knew he had only himself to blame.

"Since that visit I put the castle out of my mind, until he died and it became my responsibility. Even then I was not ready to take it on, knowing what a fortune it would cost to put it right."

"I thought you had made a fortune, old boy," Win observed languidly.

"Luckily, I had. I am going to need it to restore this place. I suppose the truth is that until now I did not care enough. Maybe I still will not."

They descended the grand staircase and explored the drawing room, which was in a better state than the passage.

The furniture which mercifully had not been removed was not only significant but looked in good repair.

The curtains, however, were torn and dirty. The carpet was threadbare and badly in need of brushing.

There were the remains of what had once been a fire in the fireplace.

But Michael felt that if the room was cleaned and

refurbished it could be a room which any gentleman could find delightful. Any lady would certainly be impressed.

That thought made him shiver. He had come here to escape from prospective brides.

He was quite certain that sooner or later Alice would follow him, determined to marry him, although he definitely harboured no wish to marry her or anyone else for that matter.

Then, as they wandered from room to room, a change came over Michael. Win watched him with interest.

Despite its shabbiness the great castle still resonated with the English history of which it had been a part for centuries. It was all around them. It was there on the walls, hung with pictures of his forebears stretching back for centuries.

It was present in the furniture that they had collected and the books that filled the library.

"It is magnificent," Michael breathed. "How can the fool who owns it have let it fall into this state?"

Win coughed delicately.

"No wish to be offensive, old boy, but the fool is you."

"So it is. Then it is for me to put matters right!"

Suddenly he turned and faced his friend, eyes blazing with eagerness.

"And by Jove, Win, that is exactly what I am going to do."

CHAPTER THREE

Neither of them had any complaint to make about the dinner. Mrs. Brooks had excelled herself and Michael made a point of sending for her to congratulate her. She beamed with happiness.

"Now," Michael said to Brooks, when Mrs. Brooks had bustled back to the kitchen, "I want you to help me to restore the castle and make it as it must have been when you first came here."

"Me, my Lord?"

"I need your memory. You must tell me exactly how things used to look."

"It were fine in those days, even though there were a lot needing to be done to it," Brooks said. "But now, as your Lordship will see, things have become worse and worse and it's going to take some time before it looks right again."

"You must engage plenty of indoor servants to carry out the cleaning," Michael ordered firmly, "and tell me where we can find men to undertake the very necessary repairs."

"There's a good firm that has been repairing the Church. They are local men and would be glad of the work."

"Splendid. Be so good as to send for them, so that we can discuss the costs."

"There is one gentleman I think you will find very

interesting, my Lord."

"Who is that?"

"Major Newton. When he retired from the Army, he took to designing gardens and very fine designs they be too. Not just flowers, but a lot of herbs and plants which us had never heard of before."

"He sounds like the kind of man that I could use. The garden looks as though no one has worried about it for years."

"No one has," Brooks agreed. "That's why you will find the Major very helpful. There be people from all over the County who asks him to advise them on their gardens."

"It seems a strange business for a soldier," Michael mused, becoming interested.

"He's not like any other soldier," Brooks added eagerly. "He's a very learned man. Sometimes even the Vicar doesn't understand a word he says."

Michael laughed.

"So the definition of a learned man is one who cannot be understood?" he said. "Well, I would like to meet him."

Brooks's eyes were shining.

"I don't believe this is really happening," he said. "Does your Lordship mean to stay here?"

"I am here to stay, at least while the work is going on, which I think will take a long time. I will send for the rest of my belongings and I am settling in for a long siege. Now, if you will be kind enough to leave us the brandy decanter, I shall not be needing you again tonight."

The two young men enjoyed a drink in the library. Michael occupied himself with looking at the books, while Win, who was musical, amused himself on the piano which, astonishingly, was still in tune.

Almost without realising what he was doing, Michael

began to hum the song he had heard that afternoon.

"I didn't know you knew that song, old boy," Win said, looking up from the keyboard.

"Do *you* know it?" Michael asked casually.

"It's an old country song. My Nanny used to sing it to me."

He began singing, accompanying himself on the piano. He had an agreeable light tenor, but he was not as pleasant to Michael's ears as the sweet voice he had heard that afternoon.

That night, as he walked upstairs to bed in the bedroom which he was told had always been used by the owner of the castle, Michael felt not only tired but excited.

He stood at the window looking out at his estate and for the first time since he had inherited the title, he felt a growing pride of ownership.

'I have won,' he said to himself. 'Or at least, I am going to win. I have never known anything like this. I feel like a King surveying his domain.'

Then he smiled wryly to himself.

'But on one thing I am resolved. There is going to be no Queen!'

Then, for no reason that he could fathom, he found himself remembering the girl by the river.

*

On the next morning Bettina was washing up the flower vases in the kitchen when she heard her father come in through the front door. At once she was aware of something different in his step, a kind of eagerness.

"I am in the kitchen, Papa," she called.

He came hurrying in and she could see the excitement in his face.

36

"What has happened?" she asked.

"I have just heard that the Earl of Danesbury has arrived at the castle. What do you think of that?"

Bettina turned away to concentrate on what she was doing in the sink lest her father see a sudden surge of colour in her face.

"That's incredible," she said.

She had not mentioned to Papa that she had caught a distant glimpse of the Earl on the previous day and had encountered his companion.

Considering the stranger's disgraceful behaviour, she supposed she ought to complain about him. But for some reason she was unwilling to discuss the matter.

"We never believed it would happen," she said now, for something to say.

"But my dear, I haven't told you the big news. Lord Danesbury wants to see me so that I can design the castle garden for him."

Bettina dropped a vase into the sink.

"Careful, my dear! Isn't that wonderful news?"

"Wonderful," she echoed in a hollow voice.

"According to Brooks he has big plans. He arrived last night, without warning, accompanied by a friend."

"What – what kind of friend, Papa?"

"My dear, how do I know? One of his London cronies, I suppose, that he brought with him lest the countryside bore him. These fashionable men always crave amusement."

"I suppose they do," she agreed in a colourless tone.

"But the important point is that he means to stay at the castle and restore it."

"He must be dreaming," Bettina observed.

"Well it is a dream that everyone around here is going

to appreciate. Do you remember me telling you that when I first lived here years ago, I fell in love with the castle gardens and painted them?"

"I do remember. And then when we came back four years ago and found them in such disarray, you completed some more pictures, showing how you thought the gardens deserved to look. I thought you were indulging in wishful thinking."

"Some wishes do come true. I might as well take them with me now."

His eyes were shining and it was clear that he was in seventh Heaven.

"Just think what this will mean," he said. "I will not conceal from you, my dear, that the money he will pay me is very much needed. You are a wonderful little housekeeper, but my Army pension is very modest and even you can only make it stretch so far.

"And everyone in the neighbourhood will benefit from the extra work that will be available. Think of the prosperity this will bring!"

That decided Bettina. Now there was no way that she could tell her father what had happened. For the sake of the village she must keep silent about the Earl's friend and his unmannerly behaviour.

Then a terrible thought struck her and her hands flew to her face.

To fend him off, she had told him that she was betrothed, thinking that he was passing through and it would not matter what he believed.

But he was staying. She might bump into him again and in this tiny place he would soon realise that what she had said was untrue.

Suppose he spread the shocking story that she had

untruthfully claimed a fiancé – something that no delicately reared female would ever do.

Then she reassured herself again. He could not recount that story without explaining his own part. Besides, he was unlikely to recognise her even if he did meet her again.

He had probably already forgotten that she existed.

Then she discovered that this thought did not please her either, which was very strange.

She knew his behaviour was shocking, but it was only her head that told her so.

For the few minutes they had talked, she had been aware of the bright sun and the glow of the beautiful countryside.

But above all she had noticed that he was extremely handsome. She had never seen such a good looking man in her whole life. Certainly not in the village.

It was like discovering another world, where men were giants instead of village boys. Somewhere, she had known that there must be such a world.

And now that she had glimpsed it, it was to be snatched away. Whoever the handsome stranger was, she would have to avoid him.

She sighed.

Life was very unfair sometimes.

*

An hour later the Major was approaching the entrance to the castle, the plans under his arms. In the light of this new hope the whole world looked different, especially the castle.

The door was open and he walked in. As he did so he saw Brooks coming up the passage.

"If this means what I hope, Brooks, then it is very good news."

"Very good indeed," Brooks agreed. "His Lordship wants to restore everything to the way it was originally."

"Please take me to his Lordship before he changes his mind."

They had been walking down the passage as they spoke. Now Brooks flung open the door of the library.

"Major Newton to see you, my Lord."

The Major stepped into the library and saw a man sitting at a table by one of the windows.

He turned round and at once the Major had a feeling that this was a man who could achieve what he wanted, simply because it was the right action at the right moment.

Michael held out his hand.

"Thank you for coming so quickly. I understand from Brooks that I will need your services and he has assured me that you can do what no one else can."

The Major smiled.

"I believe I can," he said.

Without further words the Major took his designs from under his arm and laid them out over the table.

"I think these will show you," he said, "how magnificent the castle garden looked when I first saw it. I was young at the time, but I was so thrilled with its beauty that I sat down and painted it."

"Extraordinarily well from what I can see," Michael replied turning over the pictures. "This is how I want it to look again, exactly as it does in these paintings."

The Major drew in his breath.

"I would love to make the attempt," he said. "But I must warn you, it will be very expensive."

He spoke almost nervously, half expecting Michael to beat a retreat.

But to his surprise he responded simply,

"I can afford whatever it costs and I am not prepared to skimp or cut corners. I want the garden to be as beautiful as you have shown it in your pictures.

"You have obviously known the castle far longer than I have. I want you to tell me all you know."

Delighted, the Major began to talk. He carried on talking throughout the excellent lunch Brooks served with Michael listening to him, enraptured.

By the time they were ready to return to the library Win had joined them. He had been exploring the neighbourhood and was in cheerful spirits.

"There's some good fishing to be had," he announced. "And a decent livery stable."

"I am so glad you found something to amuse you," Michael said.

"Oh, yes, a good deal. Between you and me, old fellow, there are some dashed pretty girls around here too."

The Major coughed delicately.

"Major, allow me to introduce my friend, Lord Winton Shriver, who is staying with me."

The two men shook hands cordially enough, but each knew within a few minutes that he did not find the other congenial.

To Win the Major appeared severe and stuffy. To the Major, Win appeared light-minded and trivial.

Michael summoned champagne and the three men drank.

"To the future," Michael toasted.

"Let me say, my Lord, from the bottom of my heart, welcome home," proposed the Major.

Welcome home! Those words struck Michael as exactly right. He had, indeed, come home.

He realised that he needed this man as a friend. The Major was intelligent, educated and cultivated. And, as the pictures made very plain, he was in tune with the spirit of the castle.

"Perhaps you could help me in another way," he said suddenly. "I want to introduce myself to some of my more prominent neighbours, the Mayor, the Vicar and so forth."

"Then do not forget the Lord Lieutenant of the County," the Major said with a laugh. "Sir William Lancing is a decent fellow but tends to be very conscious of his own importance. Pay him a little flattering attention and he is yours for life."

"You know him well?"

The Major laughed ruefully.

"I am obliged to attend a very boring meeting at his house every month. Nothing of importance is ever decided or even discussed, but it cheers him up."

"Thank you for the warning. I think my best course is to host a dinner party as soon as it can be arranged. Naturally I would want you to come with your wife and family."

"You are very kind. My only family is my daughter. My wife died some years ago."

"You must have found life in the Army very difficult with a young girl to raise?" Michael asked sympathetically.

"It had its problems, but my daughter and I have always been deeply attached. Her mind is quick and she has learned from me almost all I can teach her."

"I look forward to meeting her when you both come to dinner. As neither Lord Winton nor I are married, I fear we are going to be rather short of ladies."

"Can't have that!" Win said at once.

"Never fear," the Major suggested cheerfully. "The Vicar and his wife have three unmarried daughters in their twenties."

"Ah!" Michael said. "How – how very fortunate."

"Jolly good," Win added faintly.

Michael made a swift decision. He had never met Miss Newton but she was doubtless as much a lady as her father was clearly a gentleman.

"I wonder if I might ask you a favour, Major. Would your daughter oblige me by acting as my hostess? I know it is a little unconventional, but your presence will make it perfectly proper."

"Your Lordship honours us."

"Not 'your Lordship'," Michael said quickly. "Please call me Danesbury as all my friends do. I shall decide on an early date for the party. In the meantime I should like you to start hiring the men you will need."

He sat at his desk and scribbled something.

"This is a draft on my bank to cover your initial expenses."

The Major stared at the amount. For the first time he understood that this man really could afford the monumental task he had set himself.

*

The Major hurried home and found Bettina impatiently awaiting him.

"Such great news I hardly know how to tell you," he burst out. "The Earl means to restore everything, the castle, the garden, the furniture. My dear, this place will be so much better for his coming. He is everything that he should be."

"You liked him then?"

"Oh, yes, a great deal. A sensible man, a man of determination."

Bettina recalled the willowy youth she had seen briefly and concluded that he must have a store of good sense that did not appear on the surface.

"Was his friend there too, Papa?"

"Oh, yes, Lord Winton. I met him briefly. I have to tell you, my dear, that he did not impress me favourably. Pleasant enough manners, but a light and inconsequential character."

Bettina did not reply, but her mind told her that this was only what she would have expected.

"But never mind him," her father continued. "The Earl is the important one. He is moving workmen in to start the repairs. I am to hire everyone I need and he has handed me a sum of money so that I can make an immediate start."

He flourished the banker's draft.

"What do you say to that?"

Bettina read it and gulped.

"Papa! So much?"

"He is determined to do everything properly. And now I have some news that will delight you. He is planning a dinner party for the notables in this area and he wishes you to be his hostess."

"Me? But he doesn't know me."

"I have told him all about you."

"But – me? Be hostess for an Earl? Papa, are you quite mad? What would I wear?"

"What do you wear when we dine with the Vicar?"

"My 'best' evening gown is four years old and shabby. Our friends pretend not to notice but – "

"Yes, yes, I understand. You must wear a new gown and look appropriate. I shall give you some of this money for the purpose."

"Thank you Papa, but I still do not think I can be hostess to such a party."

Lord Winton would be there. He would know her again.

But if she appeared well dressed, like a grand lady, surely she could outface him?

She made one last attempt.

"There is etiquette and protocol and – and lots of formality that I know nothing about," she told her father.

"But we have dined with the Lord Lieutenant and his wife. You have seen what she does. She and the other ladies leave the men to their port after dinner. I do not believe there can be much more to it than that," he added with sublime ignorance.

Bettina ceased protesting. It was not every day that she was offered a new evening gown.

*

The next day the invitations began to go out. All over the neighbourhood, the most notable inhabitants, or at least, those who considered themselves notable, opened the magic envelopes and realised that they were among the lucky few.

Bettina treated herself to a day out in the nearby town of Carwick, where there were several good shops and dressmakers.

But as she moved from place to place, it became frustratingly evident that finding what she needed was going to prove almost impossible.

There was not enough time to have a dress made for her, unless it was simple. But Bettina wanted something very special indeed.

She had almost despaired of finding it, even in the most elegant shop she had yet tried, when she came across a dress on a long stand.

"What is that?" she breathed.

"That," said Mrs. Tandy, the shop's owner, "is my tragedy."

"It should not be tragic," Bettina sighed. "It is so beautiful."

It was a ravishing creation of black gauze shot through with thin gold stripes, laid over black silk. It was lavishly draped, ending in a huge fan train, trimmed with embroidery, depicting yellow and white roses.

Some people might consider it unsuitable for a young unmarried girl like herself. It spoke of glamour and sophistication.

But she wanted it as she had never wanted anything in her whole life.

"Why is that dress a tragedy?" she asked when Mrs. Tandy had brought it out and she had walked all round it.

"Because the lady who ordered it was very slim, as you can see. When we had made it to her measurements, the stupid woman discovered that she was pregnant. She refused to collect it or pay for it. And so I lost eighty guineas."

"Eighty guineas!" Bettina exclaimed.

"Thirty guineas of that was just for the materials and I shall not even receive payment for them. Nor can I sell it to anyone else, because who else is so slim?"

"I am – almost," Bettina mused.

She made a swift decision.

"I will pay you thirty guineas for it. I can let it out myself."

Mrs. Tandy gave a little scream at the thought of anyone else touching her precious creation. Some bargaining ensued which ended in her agreeing to let the dress out herself, so relieved was she to recover some of her money.

For another two guineas she loaned Bettina a black velvet cloak and an imitation gold necklace for the evening.

Now Bettina felt she was ready for anything.

She collected her booty two days later and bore it home, where she displayed it triumphantly to her wide-eyed father.

"My love," he gasped, "that is hardly a dress for a *debutante.*"

"But I am not a *debutante,*" Papa. "That is for Society ladies. Anyway, Mrs. Tandy has altered it to fit me and she will never take it back – and it was thirty guineas."

"Thirty guineas?"

"So I have no choice but to keep it. Besides, Papa, do we want the Lord Lieutenant's wife looking down on me as a dowdy?"

"Certainly not!" the Major replied with spirit. "You are as good as any of them and when they see you in that gown, they will all know it."

When she was finally dressed for the occasion he was forced to admit that she was magnificent.

"You look like a very great lady," he said.

"That is what I hoped. The Earl is so splendid himself that I do not want to appear dull."

"Splendid? Have you seen him yet?"

"I glimpsed him briefly the day he arrived and thought what a dandy he looked."

"I cannot say that is how he appeared to me. Ah, I think I hear the carriage."

The Earl had sent his carriage to collect them. The Major draped the velvet cloak about his daughter's shoulders and they walked out together.

On the ride to the castle Bettina savoured what was happening to her. To be the hostess for an Earl and know that she looked the part. That, she was sure, was something that could never happen to her again.

The lights were glinting in the castle as the carriage

drew up outside the great front door. The Earl had arranged it so that they would be the first to arrive.

Already Bettina could see the difference. The great doors of the castle stood open and there, silhouetted against the blazing lights within, stood two gentlemen.

One was positioned a little ahead of the other and she could see, by his tall, willowy figure that this was the man she had seen at a distance the other day.

He was dressed in white tie and tails, his beautiful fair hair brushed into an elegant style. The other man was indistinct.

Footmen came forward to open the door of the carriage and let down the steps. One of them assisted her to descend.

Then she and her father were advancing. She lowered her eyes just a little as she reached the great stone steps, raising the beautiful dress so that she could climb without tripping. With her attention thus occupied, she could not look up at the Earl until the very last moment.

She heard her father saying heartily,

"Danesbury, so good to see you again."

"Major and Miss Newton. It is an honour, madam."

Bettina sank into an elegant curtsy before him. Two hands, edged by snowy white cuffs with gold cuff links, reached forward to raise her.

She placed her own hands in them and lifted her eyes to meet his.

Time stopped.

At exactly the same moment the smiles faded from both their faces. Two pairs of eyes met each other full of shock, horror and dismay.

48

CHAPTER FOUR

"Miss – Miss Newton," Michael stammered. "Honoured, madam."

"My Lord," she replied, coolly. "My father has told me so much about you and I have greatly looked forward to this meeting."

"I too, madam – have – looked forward to our meeting."

Michael cursed himself for not handling the situation better. He had a horrible feeling that he was bumbling, but every sensible thought had disappeared from his head.

He had not seen her face until the very last moment. From a few yards away he had been aware only of her magnificence, so different from the simply dressed girl by the river.

Even now he could hardly believe that this splendid, imperious young lady was the village maiden with whom he had made so free. He was shocked to remember the rudeness with which he had stolen a kiss.

And she too remembered it. That was clear from the look she was giving him, a look in which indignation blended with satire. The wretched female was enjoying his discomfiture.

He forced himself to speak normally.

"Allow me to present my friend, Lord Winton Shriver,

madam," he said, indicating the elegant man beside him.

Win bowed over Bettina's hand with killing grace.

"Enchanted, madam," he murmured.

"The pleasure is mine, sir," Bettina said, giving him her most charming smile.

"I look forward to our better acquaintance," Win responded and kissed her hand with a theatrical air of gallantry.

By now Michael had managed to regain his composure. There was a long and difficult evening to go through.

"I owe you my sincerest thanks, madam," he said to Bettina, "for agreeing to be my hostess this evening. I asked you to come early so that I could make you familiar with the castle as it is now."

"And, of course, we wanted to meet you," Win said.

"Yes, yes, naturally," Michael said lamely. "We – er – needed to meet."

He wished the earth would open and swallow him up.

"First, allow me to show you the dining room," he said. "I would like to be assured that the arrangements meet with your approval."

In the centre of the dining room stood the long rosewood table with fourteen matching chairs around it. The finest crystal, china and silver, rescued from attic cupboards by Mrs. Brooks, were arranged at fourteen places.

Roses stretched down the centre of the table, and miniature roses adorned each place setting.

"Your father assured me that roses are your favourite flower," Michael declared.

"They are indeed," Bettina informed him with a smile. "Although I am also very partial to lilies, lilacs and hyacinths."

He had the grace to blush.

"Have you visited the castle before, Miss Newton?" he managed to ask.

"I have never ventured inside the doors."

"Then it will be my pleasure to show you around."

She took the arm he proffered and together they walked out of the room.

As soon as he felt it safe to speak, Michael murmured,

"You are the last person I expected to see."

"Evidently," she replied in a cool voice. "And I would not have come here had I known that this was the home of a rake and a libertine!"

"Will you be good enough to keep your voice down?" he muttered, smiling determinedly. "Your father has followed us out into the hall. Let us climb the stairs so that I can show you the picture gallery."

Together they mounted the broad oak staircase.

"Very well," Bettina said, "now that we have left them behind, where was I? Ah, yes, rake and libertine – "

"I think you do me a wrong with such harsh words. At least admit that they are an exaggeration."

"Not at all. I think they perfectly express the case. Perhaps there is another name for a man who assaults any girl who takes his fancy – "

"A kiss is hardly an assault."

"That depends on whether the lady is willing. If she is not, it is an assault. I was not. I believe I made that quite plain."

"Perfectly plain," he agreed, resisting the temptation to rub his cheek with the memory.

"Good. I hope you remember it the next time you want to *assault* a defenceless female."

"Defenceless?" he said in outrage. "You? Anyone less defenceless I have yet to meet. I have seen prize fighters with punches less impressive than yours."

Bettina's eyes sparkled with annoyance.

"Sir, I believe it is my duty to leave this house at once and inform the world why. Everyone around here thinks you are wonderful. What would they say if they knew you were an unprincipled seducer?"

This time he did not even bother to protest. Instead he regarded her warily.

"Are you going to tell them?"

"I have not yet decided," she replied with dignity.

"Have you told your fiancé?"

"Who?"

"The man to whom you are betrothed. You mentioned him at our last – er – meeting."

"It is as well that I have not told him," Bettina said, recovering from the slip. "Well for you, I mean."

"Is he very fearsome, madam?"

"He would destroy you, sir. He would break every bone in your body."

Michael's lips twitched.

"You mean his right hook is even harder that yours?"

"Much harder," she replied firmly.

"In that case, you are certainly right not to tell him. What a pity he is not here tonight. Will he not think it strange that you are acting as my hostess? Perhaps he will regard it as improper. I tremble at the thought."

Bettina cast him a sulphurous look.

"He will behave in a gentlemanly fashion," she asserted. "I only wish the same could be said of every man."

"I stand rebuked, madam. I ought, of course, to have

invited him here tonight and would have done so, if your father had mentioned your betrothal – "

"He knows nothing of it," Bettina said quickly.

"Ah! A secret engagement."

"Precisely."

"You have entered into a secret alliance with a man of whom your father disapproves? Fie, Miss Newton!"

Bettina drew herself up to her full height.

"I decline to discuss the matter any further, sir," she declared loftily.

"I understand the delicacy of your situation. Perhaps we should make a bargain."

She eyed him suspiciously.

"What kind of a bargain."

"Miss Newton," he said solemnly, "we each hold the other's fate in our hands and must solemnly pledge ourselves to conceal the truth at all costs."

"Indeed?"

"I will vow never to reveal your illicit love to the Major, if you will promise not to reveal my disgraceful character to the neighbourhood."

Then, seeing by her fulminating eye, that he had strained her patience to the utmost, he added hastily,

"Now I believe it is time that we rejoined the others."

Despite being so out of charity with the Earl, Bettina could not deny that she felt a slight quickening of excitement as she descended the great staircase, her hand lightly resting in his. For a thrilling moment she was the Mistress of this beautiful castle.

More carriages were beginning to arrive, the steps being pulled down by footmen and the doors opened to disgorge ladies and gentlemen dressed up in their party finery.

But none appeared as fine as the lady standing beside the Earl to greet them. They all noticed and reacted in their various ways.

The gentlemen gave her a second and third appreciative glance, reflecting that they had always known that Miss Newton was a 'dashed fine girl'.

The ladies were more doubtful. Mrs. Paxton, the Vicar's wife, felt crossly that one of her own brood or even herself, would have been more suitable. The Mayor's wife felt much the same, but more charitably.

Lady Lancing, the Lord Lieutenant's wife, was in a fury at what she considered to be an insult. She should have been the hostess and not this upstart little nobody whose father had obviously seized the chance to push her forward.

She greeted the Earl with her head imperiously high. He welcomed her graciously, but when she appeared not to notice Miss Newton, he said, with a touch of iron behind his smile,

"Of course you know Miss Newton, who has so kindly agreed to help me tonight."

Thus constrained, Lady Lancing was faced with no choice but to murmur a greeting, which Bettina returned calmly.

Michael, remembering the advice from the Major, paid Sir William much flattering attention and sent him on his way happy. Win also played his part beautifully, bowing low over every lady's hand, even the three plain daughters of the Vicar.

Plainest of all was Katherine, the eldest, spectacled, thin-faced and nearly thirty. While her two younger sisters had a tendency to simper, she had clearly resigned herself to her unmarried status. Her air was quiet, dignified and pleasant.

When the last guest had arrived and been shown into

the drawing room by Brooks, Michael murmured,

"Well done, so far, Miss Newton. To the manor born."

"But I wasn't to the manor born and Lady Lancing will never forgive me. You should have asked her, you know."

"But I would much rather have you."

As they entered the drawing room, Lady Lancing rose and addressed Michael with an air that made it plain she considered herself to be speaking for everyone.

"Lord Danesbury, we are all so glad that you have come to live amongst us."

She looked around for assent and there were dutiful nods of approval.

"We know that you will add greatly to the district," Lady Lancing continued magisterially, "and make this dear old castle as magnificent as it was in years past. Of course we realise that it will take time, but we will force ourselves to be patient, given the importance of your work."

More murmurs of assent. Then Bettina said,

"Lord Danesbury has already done an astonishing amount."

Lady Lancing's smile faded.

"You have seen it?"

"He was kind enough to show me some of the castle earlier."

It was a fatal thing to say. Lady Lancing's patience evaporated with the discovery that Bettina had already been thus privileged.

"I did not realise that visitors were already being shown round the castle," she commented icily. "In that case – "

Bowing to the inevitable Michael smiled, saying,

"We should all go at once, before the light fades."

They all trooped eagerly out into the hall.   Michael spared a moment to give Bettina a glassy stare, hissing through gritted teeth,

"It was a pity that you mentioned that point, madam."

"I was only trying to be helpful," she protested.

"Well, you can just come and help me deal with them all."

"I do not see why you should blame me for everything," she muttered, falling into step beside him. "You should have planned to show the place to everyone and not just me."

"I singled you out because you are my hostess," he growled, "and now I wish I had been struck by lightning before I ever thought of it."

"You cannot wish it more than I do," she snapped.

"Then we understand each other."

Possibly to their relief, they were afforded no further chance to converse.   Lady Lancing swooped on Michael, taking him over with a completeness that Bettina would have found insulting if she had not been so glad to be rid of him.

Win, ever soft-hearted, caught up with her and talked to her pleasantly, making sure that she was not left out, until the Major came to her rescue.

"That was so kind," said a soft voice at Win's shoulder.

Turning he looked at Katherine, smiling at him myopically through her spectacles.

"Everyone seems annoyed to find Miss Newton presiding," he said, taking her hand through his arm.

"Not everyone," she said. "Just the ladies. There is hardly a lady here who does not believe that the honour should have fallen to herself."

"Do *you* wish it ma'am?"

"Oh, no," she replied with a little shudder. "I am much

too shy. Bettina is the right person. I envy her such a forceful nature."

Win considered this remark.

"Do you know," he said at last, "I have a feeling that Michael is finding her a little too forceful."

"Why do you say that?"

"I am not sure, except that he seems uneasy in her presence. I wonder if they have met before. If so, he has never mentioned it to me."

They moved on with the rest of the party.

From room to room they all strolled, exclaiming with delight. Some rooms were now in good condition, some were being rebuilt, but Lady Lancing pronounced on all of them. Then the Mayor's wife did the same, followed by the Vicar's wife. Their husbands brought up the rear.

The only person who did not feel obliged to favour the company with her opinion was Katherine. She seemed content to walk quietly on Win's arm. Only when he asked her a direct question did she answer softly,

"I think it is all so beautiful."

"Yes, it is," he agreed. "Danesbury has thrown himself into his castle, heart and soul. I really don't think he cares for much else at the moment."

"I believe it is now time for dinner," Michael announced hastily.

In solemn state they made their way downstairs. Michael escorted Bettina to her seat at one end of the table, while he took his own at the other end. Win to his pleasure found himself sitting beside Katherine.

Michael had prepared for the evening by sending for Alfonso, his London chef, who had excelled himself.

Cream of asparagus soup was followed by salmon with Sauce Hollandaise, roast chicken, ham, cucumber sauce, chocolate mousse, pastries, ice cream, and coffee.

With every course there was a different wine in a different glass, – chambertin, champagne, sauterne and sherry.

Brooks was ecstatic, serving such a feast and supervising the new servants who had been hired, and who treated him with a flattering deference that he had almost forgotten existed.

"Just like the old days," he kept saying to anyone who would listen. "Just like the old days."

For Bettina the dinner was less of an ordeal than she had feared. With her father on one side and Katherine on the other she was partly shielded from the resentment of the other ladies. Katherine certainly bore her no ill will and spoke to her pleasantly when she could spare attention from Win on her other side.

Michael kept his eyes on her when he could, but was largely monopolised by Lady Lancing. For tonight, he supposed he would have to endure it.

At last the meal drew to a close. Lady Lancing gave her self-satisfied smile, set down her empty wine glass and took up her fan.

Astonished, Michael recognised the signs of a hostess about to signal that the ladies should retire.

But she was not the hostess. It seemed that the Lord Lieutenant's wife had simply decided to usurp Bettina's position.

Michael thought fast. He did not wish to snub Lady Lancing, but neither was he prepared to tolerate such an insult to Bettina. He began to speak again.

"Lady Lancing, in due course I shall wish to ask your advice about – "

Flattered by this appeal to her, Lady Lancing

abandoned her preparations for departure. Michael talked on about anything that came into his head. Afterwards he could not remember a single word he had said.

At last he finished,

"I look forward to consulting you at length, madam. And now, Miss Newton, I fear you have been wishing to lead the ladies into the drawing room for some minutes. Forgive me for delaying you."

Bettina answered him with a smile. Her sharp eyes had seen the little byplay and she appreciated Lord Danesbury's tactics. She rose from her chair and the other ladies followed at once. Lady Lancing, being no fool, realised how she had been outmanoeuvred and scowled. But she could do nothing but traipse after Bettina out of the room.

But in the drawing room there was nobody to protect Bettina. Lady Lancing sat down beside her and said in a hooting voice,

"Dear Miss Newton, how brave of you to make the attempt to act as his Lordship's hostess this evening."

"I was delighted to be able to assist his Lordship," Bettina answered, keeping her voice formal.

"Of course you were. We all realise that your dear Papa is vital to Lord Danesbury, who clearly cares so much for his garden. I always think that being a gardener must be the hardest work of all. But I dare say your father is used to it."

At any other time Bettina would have managed a fierce retort to this attempt to reduce her father to the status of a servant. But she could hardly create a scene in the Earl's drawing room.

Then, while she was mentally casting around for an answer, she heard an almost incredible sound.

Male laughter, coming from just outside the door.

The next moment the door opened and the Earl entered, followed by the all the other men. Instead of lingering over the port, he had waited approximately five minutes before saying,

"Shall we join the ladies, gentlemen?"

Everyone was surprised. Only Bettina guessed, or thought she had guessed, why he had done so.

He was protecting her and while she might tell herself that he was merely acting as a courteous host, she could not help her heart warming to him, just a little.

Among his other preparations for the evening Michael had arranged for the piano to be brought into the drawing room. Now Brooks raised the lid, indicating that the next part of the evening would be music making.

The Vicar, who was famous for his funny songs, tried to look modest when he was called on to perform, but yielded immediately.

Katherine accompanied him and played so beautifully that Win immediately demanded a solo from her.

Giving him a shy smile, she complied and everyone sat entranced. She was indeed a talented pianist.

Lady Lancing condescended to play and performed a short piece stiffly and correctly, in sad contrast to Katherine's inspiration.

The Vicar's two other daughters sang a duet, also accompanied by Katherine. Lady Lancing applauded their modest performance loud and long, proclaiming in her hooting voice.

"My dear Miss Newton, what a shame you never learned to play, otherwise you could have delighted us. I always say that no woman can be considered truly accomplished who does not know music."

This was so obviously ill-natured that an awkward

silence fell. Michael waited for Bettina to make a spirited riposte, but she only smiled awkwardly and said,

"Not everyone can be as accomplished as your Ladyship."

Had he but known, it cost her a huge effort to speak so mildly. Bettina's nature was neither meek nor mild. Her instinct was always to speak her mind, sometimes with disastrous frankness.

But she could not employ that frankness now. She was Lord Danesbury's hostess and must behave with decorum.

This was all Lord Danesbury's fault, she thought, forgetting that she had warmed to him a moment earlier. Why had he invited her here to be insulted?

Then she noticed that he had risen to his feet.

"Miss Newton is too modest," he said firmly. "I know her to be a superb singer."

There was a murmur of surprise. Heads turned to look at Bettina, but she was regarding Michael, her cheeks burning, her eyes reproachful.

"Miss Newton," he said, approaching her, "I once heard you sing a song I particularly love, called '*Where the sweet river wanders.*' You sang it so beautifully that I cannot rest until I hear it again. Will you delight me by singing it now? My friend knows the song and will accompany you on the piano."

"A pleasure, madam," Win said promptly and headed straight for the piano.

Michael took Bettina's hand and indicated for her to step forward. But she shook her head.

"What are you doing?" she murmured.

He leaned close enough to whisper,

"Do you think I am going to allow that woman to deride you? Come now, no shirking."

"But I cannot do this."

"Of course you can. Forget these people and sing as you sang before in a field by the river, your face upturned to the sun, your voice rising to the Heavens. *Sing it for me*."

She was about to refuse but something in his voice prevented her. His eyes were strangely kind, but they also held an intensity that told her this was important to him. He was truly angry at how she had been treated and this was his way of honouring her.

While she hesitated, his hand tightened on hers and he drew her irresistibly forward to take her place standing in front of the piano, facing the room.

Win struck up the first chords and Bettina began to sing.

"*Where the sweet river wanders,*

My love and I walked,"

Dismayed, she realised how the words recalled the day when they had met by the river, and for a moment she was almost overcome with self-consciousness.

Then she forced herself to be calm and think only of doing justice to the song.

Gradually the music and the sad words drove out all other thoughts, and she forgot everything except the joy of singing and pouring her heart into the tale of lost love.

"*And never, never be parted again.*

Never be parted,

Aye those were his words."

Now she ventured a brief glance in Michael's direction and realised that he was watching her with total attention, absolutely still.

"*But oh, life is cruel,*

And now he is gone."

Michael's eyes never left her. He seemed to be seeing something that left him thunderstruck.

"*The river still wanders,*

But I walk alone."

The last melancholy notes died away.

In the silence she ventured to glance again at Michael and saw that he wore a dazed looked, like a man being recalled unwillingly to reality.

Then he rose to his feet and led the applause. Win too was applauding her, as was everyone. Even Lady Lancing forced her hands together once or twice, not wishing to make her chagrin look too obvious.

Now Bettina knew how Michael had felt a moment ago, for she too felt as though she had spent time in another world, and was finding it hard to return to this one.

Michael was standing in front her.

"That was beautiful," he enthused. "Will you not sing for us again?"

"No," Bettina said quickly. "Thank you, but I cannot."

"I understand and you are right. We made our point very clear to them all, did we not?"

"I – I am not quite sure what point we were making."

"Oh, I think you understand very well."

He pressed her hand.

Then he turned away to his guests so quickly that she almost wondered if she had imagined it.

But she could still feel the pressure on her hand.

Katherine approached her and spoke shyly,

"That was truly beautiful, Miss Newton. I had no idea that you were so talented."

"From a true musician such as yourself, that is praise that I really value," Bettina answered her sincerely.

"I hope some of it was for me," Win said plaintively. "After all, I *did* play the accompaniment."

Katherine said,

"And very well, too, my Lord. *Such* an accompaniment!"

They all laughed and Bettina noticed how becoming laughter was to Katherine. There was a faint flush to her cheeks and an inner light seemed to glow from her as she looked up at Lord Winton.

'Oh, no!' Bettina thought. 'She must not fall in love with him. These two men are dangerous. They come to us from a different world and eventually they will return to it, leaving us behind. Katherine should be wise and keep her heart safely in her own possession – as I am determined to keep mine.'

At this part of the evening it was usual to serve tea, prior to the departure of the guests. For a moment Bettina was confused, but then Brooks appeared, directing a questioning look at Lord Danesbury.

Raising his voice a little Michael ordered pleasantly,

"Take your instructions from Miss Newton tonight, Brooks."

The butler gave her a small bow.

"Shall I serve tea now, miss?"

"Yes please, Brooks."

He walked to the door where two maids were waiting and ushered them in.

Michael immediately took Bettina's hand and led her to the sofa beside a small table, signalling with a nod that the tea should be set before her.

As the hostess it fell to her to pour and pass around the cups, which she did with the help of Katherine, who was in turn assisted by Win.

Michael grinned at the sight of his friend, the fashionable man about town, meekly doing the bidding of the Vicar's daughter.

Lady Lancing held one more card in her hand and she played it determinedly. As the evening ended and the other guests departed, she made it clear that she intended to be the last to leave.

But Michael foiled even this stratagem, presenting Bettina's attempt to depart with the words,

"Forgive me, madam, but you cannot leave yet. You are my hostess and you must bid every guest farewell."

Defeated, Lady Lancing flounced out, leaving Bettina the victor.

Under her father's eye, Michael raised her hand to his lips.

"My gratitude, madam. You were the perfect hostess."

"I fear that is more than I deserve," she replied. "But I am glad that I did not disgrace you."

"There was never any danger of that, madam."

His eyes were warm and glowing. For a moment she thought that he would kiss her hand again and drew in her breath. For some curious reason her heart was beating faster than usual.

But instead he only placed his other hand over hers, clasping it gently.

Then he led Bettina and her father out to the waiting carriage, assisted her up the steps and remained standing as they drove away.

At the bend in the road she looked back and saw him still standing there, watching.

CHAPTER FIVE

Bettina made certain that she was up early next morning. The ball was over and it was time for Cinderella to come down to earth.

That meant packing up the beautiful velvet cloak and the imitation gold necklace. They had to be returned to Mrs. Tandy today. Cinderella's finery had turned back to rags.

She permitted herself one last look back at the previous evening, when she had reigned as belle of the ball and the Earl had gallantly championed her against her enemies.

It had been a glorious evening and it would never come again. So she allowed herself just one sweet memory and then put it out of her mind. Or at least, she tried to.

Over breakfast she chatted to her father with determined cheerfulness, refusing to let him see the sad cloud that had mysteriously settled over her heart.

But he seemed completely oblivious, apparently regarding Bettina as still a child, who had been given a wonderful treat. It did not occur to him that her life had been turned upside down.

As soon as breakfast was over, she piled the precious box into the gig and set out for the nearby town.

But she had only travelled a couple of miles when she heard a voice calling from behind her.

Looking over her shoulder, she saw Michael on horseback.

She tried to ignore the way her heart suddenly started to beat harder. That was part of last night's fantasy and deserved no place in reality.

She drew the gig to a halt and Michael reined in his horse, turning the animal so that he could talk to her face to face.

"I called at your house hoping to see you," he said. "Finding you gone, I hastened to catch up. I have much to say to you."

"I think not, sir," she said with composure. "You thanked me last night."

"I have much more to say to you than that. Let me ride with you."

Before she could object, he dismounted, tied his horse to the rear of the gig and climbed in beside her.

If she was to order him away, it must be done now, but the words would not come. Surely she could allow herself just a little more of his company?

"Allow me," he asked, taking the reins from her hands.

"You do not care whether I allow you or not," she pointed out. "You just do as you wish."

"Am I still in trouble over that day by the river?" he enquired, giving the horse the signal to start. "Well, I suppose I deserve it. I behaved abominably.

"Will you not please accept my deepest apologies? I do not normally forget my manners, but you are so beautiful and charming that I was just carried away – "

"Please," she interrupted him hastily. "You must not talk to me like that."

He must not do so because the words were so sweet to her. But she dared not let him suspect it.

"No, of course not," he said hastily. "That was how I talked on that disgraceful occasion, wasn't it. I promise you, Miss Newton, the memory fills me with remorse."

This was all very proper and a lady should be delighted to hear his words.

But Bettina discovered that she was such a perverse creature that she could think only of a river bank in the sunlight, and a handsome man speaking sweet honeyed words as he took her into his arms.

"The memory also distresses me," she remarked primly. "So much so that I wish never to think about it again."

"Just answer me one question before we abandon the subject. Why, feeling thus, did you agree to be my hostess?"

"After my father agreed for me, I had little choice. Besides, I did not know that you were Lord Danesbury. I thought you were Lord Winton."

"Win? Good grief!" Michael roared with laughter. "Poor old Win."

"The fact is," she admitted, "that when I saw him on that day, he looked much grander than you."

"That is because he spends every penny on his fashion. The trouble is that his means are limited. He has a small fortune of his own, left to him by his grandmother. His father supplements it with an allowance. He is going to have to marry an heiress I fancy."

Bettina was silent, hoping that Katherine had not become too attached to Win.

It was a reminder to her that he and the Earl came from a different world to hers.

"Anyway, I consider the incident closed," she said.

"Then you will not feel it necessary to confide in your fiancé?" he asked, keeping his eyes on the road ahead.

"I shall confide in nobody because I do not wish to make a scandal."

"That is kind of you."

"No it isn't. I am not being kind – not to you, anyway."

"To whom then?"

"The people of this neighbourhood. Your arrival here means so much to them – work and prosperity. They are good, kind folk and you can give them so much that they need."

He turned his head slightly to look at her.

"And it was for them that you repaid my rudeness with kindness last night? They must mean a great deal to you."

"This place means everything to me. People here are not conniving and spiteful as they are in other places."

"It seems to me that there was plenty of spite and conniving last night," he observed mildly.

"You mean Lady Lancing? Well, you saved me from her. Besides, she is not what I meant. She is a *Ladyship*."

"You mean you expect the worst from anyone with a title? Well, I suppose I can understand that."

"Will you take the next turning onto the Carwick road, please?" Bettina asked, refusing to be drawn on this subject again.

"I don't believe I have ever been there," he mused. "I may have passed through when I was younger, but I do not remember."

"It is a small town, but there are a few good shops." Bettina added determinedly, "I am going to return the cloak and necklace that I hired for last night."

"They suited you admirably. I thought how splendid you looked when you walked into the castle. I simply did not recognise you as the girl I had met earlier. And then when I did – what a shock you gave me!"

He began to laugh and after a moment she joined in.

"You could not have been more horrified than I was," she said.

When they reached the shop, she begged him to remain outside while she walked in. She did not feel she could bear having him watch her hand everything back. She was quite sure that the London Society ladies he knew would never need to do such a thing.

When she emerged from the shop she discovered that the Earl had vanished. A street urchin was holding the head of the horse.

"The gentleman said he'd be back soon and you was to wait for him over there," the urchin declared, pointing to a tea shop that stood on the corner.

The tea shop was as dainty as a lace handkerchief. Bettina found a seat in the window, from where she could watch the street. She ordered some tea and sat waiting for the Earl wondering what had delayed him.

When he finally entered she thought how incongruously vital and masculine he looked in these surroundings. It was an effort not to smile at him in sheer joy at his presence.

"Forgive me," he said, seating himself. "I should not have run off like that, but an idea came to me and I wanted to surprise you."

He broke off to order more tea from a little waitress in a snow-white lacy apron.

"Surprise me?" Bettina asked.

"I still haven't thanked you properly for the help you gave me last night."

"There is no need – "

"I think there is. Please, Miss Newton, allow me to finish."

"I beg your pardon, sir."

"Then will you please accept this with my thanks."

He handed a small packet across the table to her. It was neatly wrapped in gold paper and tied with satin ribbon.

Slowly she opened it and discovered inside an exquisite locket on a fine chain.

Lifting it carefully she realised at once that it was solid gold and very valuable, although its value was nothing beside its beauty. She had never seen anything so lovely in her life.

But loveliest of all was the fact that *he* had given it to her.

And that was exactly why she could not accept it.

For a moment all her good resolutions tottered. She had vowed to be strong, not to admit, even to herself, that she was falling in love with him. But could she not accept this one gift, to treasure in the years to come?

The waitress arrived with the fresh tea. As she fussed about the table, Michael tried to keep his eyes on Bettina's face.

If only this interruption had happened later, he thought. It was somehow important to watch Bettina and try to read her thoughts.

He thought he saw a flicker of pleasure in her eyes, but it was gone in a moment and a sadness seemed to settle over her.

At last the waitress left them. Bettina's face, he was dismayed to see, was still sad.

"Don't you like it?" he asked gently. "I can change it for something else."

"No, it is *so* beautiful," she said quickly. "I love it but – I cannot accept it."

"Why not?"

"Surely I do not have to explain? I could never accept such a gift, so valuable – it would not be – proper."

"But may I not thank you for your kindness."

"Not with something like this. I could never wear anything so fine. You should give this to some great lady. I am just an ordinary country girl."

"I do not think you are ordinary at all," he responded gravely.

She blushed and shook her head.

Michael was again overwhelmed by the same feeling that had made him kiss her by the river. If they had been alone he might have yielded to it, but in this place all he could do was watch her wistfully.

"Please," he said, "will you not reconsider?"

"I could not accept it. How could I ever explain it to anyone?"

"You mean to your fiancé? He would object?"

"Of course he would," she declared, clutching at straws. "He would be scandalised. He might even call you out."

"I see. In that case, I will not try to change your mind. Please believe that I did not intend anything improper."

"I know you didn't. You meant only to be kind, but you see how it is in this place, how much resentment there was when you singled me out to be your hostess. Everyone knew that it was not right."

"That is for me to say," Michael declared with a touch of arrogance. "If I choose you to head my table, it is nobody else's business."

Her wry smile brought him back to his senses.

"I am sorry," he said. "My poor girl, it was you who paid the price, wasn't it?"

"Well, you did take care of me very well. But you

should really have asked Lady Lancing!"

"That dreadful woman!"

Bettina's lips twitched.

"She is, isn't she?" she asked longingly. "Oh, I know it's uncharitable to say it – "

"It's not uncharitable at all. It is a plain statement of fact. A more appalling creature I never met."

"Surely you must have met worse in London?" Bettina asked innocently.

"I don't think I have met worse in the entire world," he confided.

They laughed together.

This was better, Bettina thought. She might allow herself to enjoy these moments of camaraderie and keep them to look back on.

Gently she pushed the box with the pendant back across the table.

"Please," she said.

Without a word he put the box into his pocket.

"I ought to be going home," Bettina said. "I have a lot of work to do."

Michael thought of her as he had seen her last night in all her magnificence. And he thought of her kneeling by the river, cutting reeds, so fresh and simple. And he could not decide which picture he liked more.

But it displeased him to think of her having to do rough work.

When they left the tea shop he said to Bettina,

"I have a small errand to run. Please wait for me by the gig."

She did so and saw him return a few minutes later, his arms filled with flowers.

"You cannot refuse to let me give you these," he said.

"No, I will not refuse them," she replied gladly.

When she was settled into the gig he piled all the flowers into her arms. The heady scent of them was intoxicating and she sensed that she would remember this moment as long as she lived.

Michael tossed a coin to the urchin who grinned at the amount and fled.

A few minutes driving brought them back into the country, where the elderly pony trotted at an easy pace on the road that led back to Hedgeworth.

"I am so delighted you have accepted something from me," Michael said. "And you will not need to explain these to your fiancé, because they will be dead before you see him again. Unless, of course, he arrives tomorrow."

"No, he won't do that," Bettina said quickly.

"Perhaps he is in some profession that keeps him away? The Army? No, of course not. Your father would hardly disapprove of a man in his own walk of life."

"I did not say my father disapproved of him."

"Then why the secrecy?"

"Please – "

"Forgive me. It is none of my concern. But I hope he is worthy of you, Miss Newton. If he is, he must be a very fine man indeed."

"You are too kind to say so," she replied in a voice so low that he had to strain to hear her.

Nothing more was said on the journey home, both of them being occupied with their own thoughts.

Neither of them had remembered that it was the custom, after a dinner party, to call upon the hostess with thanks.

Since the host and hostess lived apart, it was unanimously decided by the guests, that the Earl should receive the visit. After all, it had been his party and nobody was going to resist the chance to pay another visit to an Earl.

The result was that the ladies who had been present the night before, led by Lady Lancing, attended the castle in strength and were informed by Brooks that his Lordship was out but would return soon. If they would care to wait –

They were delighted to wait and to look around while they did so. They examined every piece of furniture, every carpet, every window.

And that was how, looking down the steep road that led to the village, they saw the gig arrive at the Major's house.

They saw the Earl driving, with Bettina beside him, her arms full of flowers. They saw him jump to the ground and unhitch his own horse from behind the gig.

They saw him mount and then reach out to take her hand and carry it respectfully to his lips, before galloping away.

They saw Bettina sit gazing after him, with an expression on her face that they were too far away to see and could therefore speculate pleasurably and endlessly about her.

What they could be sure of was that she sat there, quite still, for a long time, before turning the gig in at the gate.

"Well!" exclaimed Lady Lancing.

*

It was Lady Lancing who insisted that, as Bettina had been the hostess, she too must receive a call. But not from everyone. Only from herself.

Accordingly, she arrived in state at the Major's house that same afternoon. With huge formality she paid 'her respects', while Bettina listened, wondering what her visitor had really come to say.

She was soon left in no doubt.

"I greatly admired your spirit, Miss Newton, in taking on a role to which you are hardly accustomed. In the circumstances I think I may say that you acquitted yourself creditably."

"Your Ladyship is too kind," Bettina murmured, with an irony that she knew would pass unnoticed.

"It is good of you to say so. I believe I am known for the generosity of my nature. And therefore I feel it will not come amiss if I venture to put you on your guard."

At this, Bettina's eyes flashed a warning, but her guest was too absorbed in herself to notice.

"Of course I know that it is hardly necessary with you, Miss Newton. Your behaviour is always so proper, your manners so delicate."

"In that case – "

"But Lord Danesbury is so affable, is he not, so generally pleasing? And he always knows, does he not, how to make the perfect gesture?"

As she spoke she indicated the flowers, which by now Bettina had arranged in two vases.

Bettina hesitated, unsure what to say, but Lady Lancing was charging on.

"You must not deny it, you know," she said roguishly. "It is only natural that his Lordship should wish to take you for a drive and give you flowers, since you stood in for the lady who would normally have been his hostess. I wonder exactly what her name is."

This was a shot in the dark. Lady Lancing had no knowledge of any lady, but she had deduced the likelihood of such a person and was too clever to overstate her case.

She waited to see if Bettina would respond, but, being disappointed, she continued,

"Well, no matter. She is sure to be somebody wealthy, beautiful and titled. Naturally he does not wish to show her the castle while it is still in some disarray, so he makes do with whoever is available."

Bettina ground her nails into her palm, but refused to be outwardly provoked.

"Such a lovely evening for you," Lady Lancing resumed, refusing to be beaten by Bettina's silence. "And of course you are far too sensible to read into it more than his Lordship intended. I know I need only drop you a hint.

"Goodness, is that the time? I really must be hurrying away. My husband has so many really important events to attend in the County, for which he needs my assistance."

Bettina rose stiffly and accompanied her to the door, watching until her enemy was out of sight.

Now she could allow herself to relax. She felt as though she were aching all over from the effort of holding herself in, refusing to respond to spite.

It had all been needless. She had always known that the Earl would never look at her, except casually.

This was not the first time that she had endured Lady Lancing's barbs, but last night had been different. Last night the Earl had been there to protect her, as he never would be again.

She felt as if she was suffocating.

Slowly she made her way back into the house, to where the Earl's flowers glowed, a riot of beautiful colour in a world suddenly become dreary.

She buried her face against the red roses and when she withdrew, they were wet with her tears.

*

The next three weeks were exciting for the whole neighbourhood.

No one could speak of anything but the restoration of the castle and gardens.

The Earl made several visits to the Major's home to discuss the plans or just to enjoy his new friendship. But, by some strange chance, Bettina was always on the point of leaving the house when he arrived.

Once the Major invited Michael and Win to dinner. Bettina played her part of the hostess to perfection, leaving the three men to their port and sitting in solitary state until they joined her. This they did, very quickly.

She then devoted all her attention to Win, even persuading him to play the piano while she listened, apparently too enraptured to turn her gaze on Michael, who glanced at her frequently.

Nor did she remain until the end of the evening, but retired early, pleading a headache.

In the quietness of her room she burrowed under the pillows, repeating to herself,

"I am not in love with him. *I am not.* And even if I was, I would *die* rather than allow anyone to suspect."

The following morning her father reproved her gently for deserting their guests, but was silenced by the pale, wan face she turned on him.

Yet it was rare for her to appear sad. Most of the time she concealed her feelings so successfully that he was able to forget everything but the work that he loved.

"I think I am dreaming," the Major said one evening after he had been at the castle all day. "Everything I have suggested to the Earl, he has agreed to and he places no restrictions on how much I can spend."

He laughed.

"People in the village say he must be getting married and he is preparing a home for his intended."

"Do *you* think so?" Bettina asked, speaking a touch more sharply than she meant to.

"Of course not. If he had a fiancée she would have been his hostess at the dinner party, not you. And she would have been down here by this time, to look the place over and tell him he had better do things her way."

"Yes," Bettina agreed, not looking at her father. "I am sure you are right."

When he had left she stood gazing out into the sunlit garden with eyes that saw nothing.

Instead she was looking at a picture she always carried in her head – herself in her magnificent evening dress, the look in the Earl's eyes when he had seen her and then another look as he remembered what had happened between them.

The thought was very sweet and almost as sweet was the memory of how she had spent the evening by his side. She still clung to that memory, even while she told herself that she should put it well aside.

Lady Lancing had first introduced the hideous possibility that there might be another woman in London with the right to claim him. Now her father had mentioned it too and it had cast a chill over her heart.

But, as he had said, if there was any such woman, she would have been present on that night.

She tried to believe that that was the end of it.

But in her heart she knew that one day it would happen, and she would see herself as she really was – a raw country girl who had briefly walked beside him, but recognised that he was not for her.

CHAPTER SIX

Michael was enjoying himself more than at any time in his entire life.

The rooms in the castle were being restored to their old beauty. The windows were being painted and the broken and dirty panes of glass were being removed.

He was so happy with what he was doing that he managed to banish London right out of his mind.

Until one day, when he was working high up on the tower, he looked down and noticed a very smart carriage drawn by four horses driving through the village.

Then as the carriage reached the gates to his drive, he drew in his breath.

He knew, almost as if a shot had been fired from a gun, whose carriage it was and who would be inside.

Alice had come searching for him.

He stepped back sharply from the edge.

For a mad moment he was tempted to send someone down with a message saying that he was not at home, sending her away.

Then he realised that he could not insult her in such a fashion.

'Dammit!' he muttered.

He left the roof of the castle and rushed to his chamber

to strip off his workmen's clothes, wash and don the kind of elegant attire Alice would expect to see him wearing.

He had barely finished when Brooks came to announce Lady Alice's arrival.

As he expected, she had been shown into the drawing room which was already looking very different from the way it had been when Michael first arrived.

Already new curtains had been put up at the windows, the whole room had been cleaned and there were plenty of flowers sent by the Major.

When Michael entered the room, Alice was standing by the window looking out into the garden. She had taken off her hat which she was holding in one hand.

He thought she looked exceedingly pretty and any other man would probably fall at her feet. Unfortunately, he was the one she wanted.

As he shut the door she ran towards him, smiling, her arms outstretched.

"Michael! Michael your castle is magnificent. I did not realise how large it is. I understand now why you disappeared, but I thought I would never see you again."

She flung herself against him so that he was obliged to put his arms round her to hold her steady.

"I had no idea where you had gone," she simpered. "How could you be so cruel as to vanish completely?"

She was clinging to him as she spoke and her lips were obviously waiting for his lips.

Taking her firmly by the arms, Michael held her away from him and said,

"You had no right to come here until I invited you. I wanted the place to be completed before you or anyone else saw it."

The next moment he realised his mistake for a smile lit

up her face and she burst out,

"So you are doing all this for me!"

"No," he said with a touch of desperation. Not for you or anyone but myself. I simply do not want anyone to see my castle until it has become a home I can be proud of. Until then, I hoped no one would know where I was."

"But darling, I am different from anyone else," Alice murmured. "I was almost distracted when I found you had disappeared from London without telling me and without leaving an address."

"How did you know where I had gone?"

Her reply was a teasing little giggle that set his teeth on edge.

"I am not going to tell you that, because you will be angry with the person who disobeyed your orders. I will only say that it took a lot of coaxing before I learnt you had come here."

So she had bribed one of his footmen, he thought grimly.

"Oh, darling, this place is so wonderful," she breathed. "I never imagined your ancestral halls would be so huge. So please take me round and show me everything. I think you are you are very, very clever."

Something possessive in her voice and in her eyes froze his blood.

He had fled London to get away from her, but suddenly he was as trapped as ever.

"You must forgive me if I decline," he said, wondering if it was possible for any refusal to make an impact on her. "It is far too soon for anyone to tour the castle."

"Oh, but darling, you must let me help you. This is something we must do together."

She smiled shyly as she added,

"I have brought some clothes so that I can stay for awhile."

She gave him an arch look, which told him, even better than words, how determined she was.

"I am afraid that is impossible," he said frantically. "You have no chaperone and it would ruin your reputation."

"Let me worry about that," Alice giggled. "Nobody knew you were here, so they will not know if I am here too."

Michael drew in a sharp breath.

He needed to get her out of here fast. If she stayed for even a few hours he would be lost.

Quite suddenly he knew the answer.

"Just wait here," he told Alice. "I have one or two orders I must give before I can talk to you."

He walked across the room as he spoke and opened the door, moving so quickly that it was impossible for Alice to stop him or to accompany him.

In a moment he was in the garden, running towards the place where he knew the Major would be working today. When the Major saw him he rose quickly to his feet.

"Good grief, Danesbury, whatever has happened? Is the castle on fire?"

"Worse than that," Michael fervently. "Women!"

"Oh, them!"

"It's all very well for you to say 'Oh, them!' You are not threatened with disaster."

"Would disaster have arrived in the form of the lady whose carriage drove up half an hour ago?"

"It certainly would. That is Lady Alice Randall, who – who – "

"Has designs on you?"

"At the risk of sounding like a conceited popinjay, yes.

She was not supposed to know I was here. Anyway, she has now turned up and shows every sign of digging in."

"How can I help?"

"Allow me to bring her to your house for lunch."

"Of course, but we do not keep the sort of larder that can provide for such a guest."

"Not to worry. Alfonso can do the cooking and I will send Brooks down with provisions. I do not wish to put you or Bettina to any of that kind of trouble. All I need is the protection of your roof."

"Then it's yours. But will the lady not think it strange?"

"She can think what she likes," Michael growled, "as long as I can escape this intrusion still a bachelor!"

"I was only thinking that I should go into town for supplies this afternoon, so we really need to have a talk before I go. That is why you are having lunch with me and it cannot be postponed."

"Good man!" Michael exclaimed in relief.

He ran back to the castle and stopped first in the kitchen to give Alfonso and Mr. and Mrs. Brooks their instructions. Then he rejoined Alice.

She glowered at him in a way that made her displeasure plain. But he pretended not to notice.

"We are having lunch with Major Newton and his daughter," he declared with a cheerfulness that he hoped did not sound too forced.

"But I want to be alone with you," Alice pouted. "I have so much to tell you and so much to hear."

"I am afraid I cannot delay this lunch," Michael said, inwardly giving thanks for Major Newton's fertile mind. "The Major is reorganising the garden, and we had planned a conference over lunch that simply cannot be postponed."

"Oh, but I am sure it could."

"No, because he is going to buy more supplies this afternoon and we have details to discuss first."

"Nonsense! What does it matter when your gardener buys things?"

Michael's eyes hardened with annoyance.

"He is not 'my gardener', but a learned and cultivated man, who I am proud to call my friend. He is a gentleman and his daughter is a lady."

Wisely she read the warning in his face and said no more, following him meekly out to her carriage. But when she had climbed in and he was beside her, she showed that she was not defeated by slipping her hand into his.

"How could you go away without telling me where you were going?" she asked again. "Everyone was astonished when you just vanished."

"I don't suppose anyone missed me," Michael intoned.

"*I* missed you," Alice replied in a soft voice. "I missed you terribly. I could not understand what had happened. But now, of course, I understand why you came here."

She obviously wanted Michael to ask what she meant. Instead, he called to the driver,

"Turn right and then left and it's the last house at the end of the lane."

The Major's house came into sight. As the carriage pulled up outside, Michael looked frantically for any sign of Bettina, but he could see no sign of anyone.

When he knocked on the door Mrs. Gates opened it.

"Miss Bettina, my Lord?" she said when he had asked her, "she is working in the garden."

"Perhaps I could bring my guest inside."

"Certainly, my Lord. Shall I fetch Miss Bettina."

"No, thank you," he said hurriedly. "I will find her myself."

There was a disdainful look on Alice's face as Michael handed her down and led her inside. This modest dwelling was not at all her idea of how ladies and gentlemen should live.

Mrs. Gates showed them into the drawing room and hurried away to make tea.

"I must leave you for a moment," Michael said hurriedly. "I shall be back directly."

He rushed away before Alice could protest and ran out into the garden in urgent search of Bettina.

He saw her almost at once, coming towards him through the flower beds.

She was carrying flowers and was surrounded by beautiful blooms. Most of them were white and her dress was also white.

He could not help thinking she looked exactly like an angel who had dropped down from Heaven.

Her fair hair shone in the sunshine and appeared to be like gold.

He had never seen her so lovely.

She stopped when she noticed him and he saw, with a sinking heart, that she was reluctant to speak to him.

He had observed how she had avoided him recently and had wondered if she did so out of loyalty to her fiancé.

But at the same time, he was not quite sure that her fiancé really existed.

She had mentioned the man in anger, but afterwards had seemed a little vague about him. Michael had come to hope that she would trust him enough to admit that there was indeed no such fiancé.

Now he hastened to reach her before she could leave.

"Miss Newton," he said urgently, "I realise that you would rather meet any man but me, but I beg you not to turn away from me. I need your help desperately."

A strange expression passed over her face, but she replied calmly,

"How can I help you, my Lord?"

"It is a question of – a lady."

Bettina grew still. This was it – of course there *was* a lady. She had been warned but tried to pretend it was not true.

"Yes?" she questioned quietly.

"Her name is Lady Alice Randall," Michael said. "She is the daughter of Earl Randall."

An Earl's daughter. Lady Lancing had warned her.

"Lord Randall is an influential man," Michael continued, hesitating because he was beginning to realise that his story would be a hard one to tell.

How did you ask one woman to protect you from another without dying of embarrassment?

"He is not really as influential as he thinks he is," he blurted out. "But he is known at Court and has the Queen's ear."

'And of course the Earl would be a courtier, needing to stand well with the Queen,' Bettina thought.

A pain was growing in her heart and it was not entirely connected with knowing that he was to marry another woman.

She realised what Michael was trying to say. Lady Alice Randall was his chosen bride. He could not afford to offend her, or her influential family, or the Queen.

So none of them must know about his dalliance with herself. He wanted her to promise to keep silent.

Anger flared in her. So he was a little man after all, so

much less than she had believed. He had amused himself and now he was scuttling for cover under her protection.

She was aware of a new feeling for him, something that was perilously close to contempt.

"There is no need to say more, my Lord," she told him. "I understand perfectly."

"You do?"

Michael stared, noticing the hint of scorn in her face and at a loss to understand it.

"When is your engagement to Lady Alice to be announced, or – " her lips curled slightly, "has it already been announced?"

For a moment he stared at her in thunderstruck silence. Then he bellowed,

"*Oh, Heavens! Not you too?*"

This explosive retort took Bettina by surprise.

"What do you mean?" she faltered.

"It seems as though the whole world is conspiring to force me to marry that woman," he cried distractedly.

Bettina began to see that she had been mistaken. The tone in which he said, '*that woman*' eased her heart.

"But not you," Michael resumed. "I thought you were the one person I might rely on to help me, but when I come to you for help, *you* see me as her property as well. I cannot bear this. I will lose my mind, I know I will!"

"But what kind of help do you need?" Bettina asked, half laughing in her relief. The world was becoming a good place again, because he was a good man. That was all she asked.

Impulsively she seized his hands.

"I will do anything you want to help you. But you must tell me what I can do."

"Alice is determined to marry me. It is unchivalrous to say so, I know. But it's true. She constantly tries to back me into corners from which there is no escape. So I fled to the country, but now she has discovered where I am and has pursued me. She plans to stay the night at the castle, unless I can prevent her."

"What?" Bettina cried out, aghast. "But how can a woman simply move in on a man like that? What about her reputation?"

"I have pointed out the dangers, but she insists on speaking as though we are engaged."

Bettina stood back and regarded him wryly.

"And we are *not* engaged," he asserted firmly, answering the expression in her eyes. "Why would I run from here if we were? I have managed to move her out of the castle by bringing her to this house.

"I have told her that I have arranged a vital luncheon meeting with your father, who has agreed to back me up, but it is your support that I really need."

"I don't understand."

"I know you are still angry with me, but I beg you not to let her see it. I need for us to appear the best of friends. I will not impose on your kindness or expect you to speak to me afterwards if you do not want to. But for pity's sake help me to discourage Alice."

Bettina was silent for a long time and he frowned, puzzled.

"You will not help me?" he asked her at last.

"I will but – I need to know exactly what I am doing. Why does this young woman feel so sure that she is engaged to you? Have you not given her some reason or hint?"

"Never knowingly or intentionally. It is all in her head and due to her parents' machinations."

"You have never proposed to her?"

"Never."

"Will you give me your word that you are not playing her false?"

For a moment Michael was angry. Who was this girl to question his honour?

Then his anger died. He should have expected this, knowing how she disapproved of him.

"I swear to you that my honour is not involved with this lady," he said. "I am not betraying her, and I have no obligations to her. It is all in her mind, but she will trap me if you do not give me your support."

To his surprise Bettina became very pale.

"Very well, my Lord. I will do whatever you wish."

"Then come into the house with me now."

"Yes indeed, I have a lunch to prepare."

"No, the food is coming from the castle. Just keep close by me and do not leave me alone with her. Your father will be back soon."

"And then he can take over 'guard duty'?" she added with a little smile.

"Something like that," he agreed.

As they spoke they had been walking back to the house and entered through the main door, going straight into the dining room.

Alice was standing by the window looking at the flowers and Michael could tell at once that she was annoyed at being kept waiting.

"I wondered what was keeping you," she said sharply as they came through the door.

"I went to find our hostess. Lady Alice, please let me introduce Miss Bettina Newton. She and her father have become my good friends since I have been at the castle."

Alice managed a strained smile and her eyes flickered over Bettina. But, after one moment's automatic suspicion, she showed no alarm.

'She is not worried by me,' Bettina thought. 'In her eyes I am probably little more than a servant. And in his eyes too, I dare say, even though he needs me now. I must not allow myself to forget that.'

Michael began to talk determinedly about the castle garden and the Major's prowess and everything the Major was doing for him.

"He has promised me the finest garden in the County," he declared, "so you will understand how important it is for us to talk together and how deeply we are both involved in the works."

"Everyone in the neighbourhood is so thrilled that Lord Danesbury is now amongst us," Bettina intervened gamely. "It will be wonderful for the castle to be restored to its former glory. We all thought it would never happen and now it is like a dream come true. Sometimes we need to pinch ourselves to believe it."

Michael smiled.

"I promise you, you can believe it. But there is a great deal to do and never enough time."

Bettina gave a laugh which she tried to make natural.

"So we can count on you not to run away in the middle of your works?" she asked the Earl pointedly.

"I promise not to do that," he replied.

Alice could endure no more. She broke in sharply,

"You may be making everyone down here in the depths of the country delighted with what you are doing, but you are neglecting your friends in London, including me."

She looked angry as she continued,

"Frankly, none of us can see the point of rebuilding a castle which is falling down."

Before Michael could speak, Bettina gave a cry.

"Oh, you must not say that," she parried. "It means so much to us and we are all thrilled and delighted that his Lordship has come to the castle."

"I really cannot think the place matters *that* much," Alice retorted scathingly. "As I just said Michael's friends in London are missing him. We all think it is time he returned."

Bettina stared at her before saying,

"But we will miss him too. We need him here."

There was an expression on Alice's face which told Michael that she was going to say something unpleasant.

He therefore spoke quickly and rather loudly.

"Let us concentrate on thanking the owner of this charming house and wonderful garden. Although he has not yet joined us, we will drink his health in his own wine."

He handed the two women a glass each as he spoke and took one himself.

Then before Alice could say anything, he lifted his glass and toasted,

"To the castle. May it bring happiness and wealth to the village and make all those who live here feel proud."

Raising her glass, Bettina said to Michael,

"You are magnificent! The whole village will look on you as their saviour."

There was such sweet fervour in her voice that Michael felt a sensation surge through him. She spoke like that when the welfare of the village was concerned. To himself she showed only coldness, but for her friends she would do anything – even if it meant associating with *him*.

He lifted his glass and replied,

"Thank you from the bottom of my heart and I hope I

will be as successful as you believe I am going to be."

"I am sure you will be," Bettina replied. "Already we are very proud of you."

Alice raised her glass and managed a smile, but it was clearly an effort and when she spoke she sounded as though her teeth were on edge.

"How nice to know that you are so appreciated, Michael. And, as you say, this house and garden are charming, so much so that I would like to see what the Major has achieved. Why don't you take me outside and show me everything?"

"It is very well worth seeing," Michael said. "But I think the person who should show you around is Miss Newton. After all, it's her garden."

"But I want *you* to show it to me," Alice pouted. "Miss Newton will not mind, I am sure."

Michael's urgent eyes sought Bettina's.

The message was unmistakable.

'*Don't desert me now.*'

"Oh, but I *would* mind," Bettina breathed. "I am so proud of the garden that Papa and I have created together, that I simply must have the pleasure of showing it to you."

"That is most kind of you," Alice began, "but I – "

"*I know!*" Bettina seemed to have been struck by a blinding inspiration. "We will all go together." She clapped her hands like a child. "Won't that be nice?"

"Delightful," Alice answered in a hollow voice.

"In that case, ladies, it will be my pleasure to escort you both," Michael declared with a fervour that barely concealed his relief.

He offered them an arm each and the three of them processed out into the garden.

CHAPTER SEVEN

The next half hour took all of Bettina's ingenuity. Having failed to dislodge her, Alice accepted her presence with poor grace and clung to Michael like a limpet.

Bettina acted as their guide, pointing out one bloom after another, while Alice kept saying, "isn't that lovely, darling?"

Michael winced every time she called him 'darling', but Bettina supposed he could hardly reprove her in the presence of a third person, however much he might want to.

It was clear that he was telling the truth when he had said he did not want to marry Alice, but Bettina would have given much to know what there had once been between them.

Ignorant of fashionable Society, she could hardly imagine that Alice had become so sure the Earl owed her a proposal of marriage without some encouragement from him.

She tried not to feel jealous, but it was hard when she regarded Alice's luxurious clothes, so different from her own simple white dress.

The young lady wore a promenade costume that was the last word in elegance. It was made of a finely-ribbed silk called faille, in a deep violet with an over-dress of blue and white striped silk, trimmed with white lace.

Perched atop Alice's dark hair was a velvet hat in matching violet, decorated with white flowers. Against her brunette beauty the effect was ravishing, and Bettina wondered how the Earl could possibly be immune to it.

Every giggle Alice gave, every proprietary tug on his arm and every repeated 'darling' coursed through Bettina painfully and made her wonder why she had ever agreed to help Michael.

"He is such a clever man, your father," Alice gushed. "And you, darling, are clever too, for having hired him to create your garden."

The word 'hired' made Michael wince again, for he was too much in awe of the Major's learning to regard him as a hired hand.

"I am really looking forward to meeting your father, Bettina," Lady Alice enthused. "I must tell him all my favourite flowers so that he will know what to plant in the castle grounds."

"Miss Newton is almost as great an expert as her father," Michael intervened, stressing the first two words to indicate his disapproval of this rudeness.

"Then I can tell her instead," Alice said. "You will act as my deputy, won't you Bettina, and make sure everything is as I like it?"

"My father does not permit me to interfere with his projects," Bettina responded with composure. "And I believe that Lord Danesbury has already settled the castle gardens with him."

"Oh, but all that has changed now I am here," Alice said with a silvery laugh.

"No," Michael said quietly, "it is not!"

"Darling, of course it is. You want me to like the castle and the grounds, don't you?"

"I want everyone to like them," he said, doggedly refusing to react to her lures.

"Oh, you know what I mean."

Suddenly Alice giggled. Bettina had the feeling that the noise set Michael's teeth on edge. She knew just how he felt.

Alice pulled Michael's head nearer to hers and whispered something in his ear, which Bettina just managed to catch.

"Why don't we tell her? It'll be such fun."

"Because there is nothing to tell," Michael replied in a firm, quiet voice.

Then he spoke more loudly.

"Miss Newton, do you know exactly when your father will be home?"

"At any moment, I believe. Do you wish to see more of the garden?"

"No, Lord Danesbury and I are going back inside," Alice announced, cross at being thwarted. "I expect you will find something to do out here."

"As a good hostess, Miss Newton will naturally accompany us indoors," Michael said at once.

So they returned to the house, each holding one of his arms and no more in accord than they had been when they had set out.

The atmosphere continued to be strained and it was a relief when the door opened and the Major entered the room.

"Papa!" Bettina exclaimed in relief.

"I have brought two more guests," he said cheerfully.

Then the others saw Win and Katherine, coming in behind him.

"Lord Winton and Miss Paxton were taking a stroll in

the castle grounds," he said. "So I invited them to come and join us."

Alice stared at the sight of Win and recognised that his presence might be useful.

"Good afternoon, Lord Winton," she said, giving him her most ravishing smile.

"Good afternoon, Lady Alice. Allow me to introduce Miss Katherine Paxton, whose father is the Vicar of Hedgeworth."

Alice greeted Katherine coolly, but found that nothing that she did could discompose the Vicar's daughter. Katherine was impeccably polite, as from some mysterious source she had found a calm self-confidence that no one could disturb.

"Win, come and talk to me," Alice purred, stretching out and taking his hand.

"By Jove, yes," he said, taking her hand, but holding on to Katherine with his other hand, in a scenario that, had he known it, was a duplicate of the one earlier.

But Alice recognised the echo and she had endured as much as she could stand. She tightened her grip on Win's hand.

"Miss Paxton will not mind my taking you away, I am sure," she hissed through gritted teeth.

"Of course," Katherine agreed at once. "I must see if I can help my hostess."

She bustled away. Evidently the thought of leaving Lord Winton with Alice held no terrors for her.

"May I assist you?" she murmured to Bettina.

"Thank you, but I don't think I am going to have to do anything," Bettina said. "Look out there."

Through the windows they could see a procession beginning to arrive outside. The Earl's chef made a stately entrance and took over the kitchen.

Bettina, trying to lay the table, found herself forestalled by Brooks, whose minions had transported china, glasses and cutlery from the castle.

Alice glanced into the room and watched the proceedings with narrowed eyes. Bettina guessed what she was thinking. Why could this lunch not have taken place at the castle?

And since Alice was not a stupid woman, the answer was bound to occur to her.

And then, just when it seemed that the atmosphere could hardly become tenser, another guest arrived.

Lady Lancing had called at the castle in search of the Earl. Hearing that he was at the Major's house, she had pursued him thence.

She arrived in haughty state and was immediately aflutter at being introduced to Lady Alice Randall, the daughter of an Earl.

Her sharp eyes took in everything, especially the possessive looks that Alice was giving Michael.

Lady Lancing was not an intelligent woman, but she possessed a cynical shrewdness that served her well in this situation. She knew now why the Earl had fled to the castle from London, she guessed why Lady Alice had pursued him and she heartily wished her well.

If she could only see the Earl trapped into matrimony by a woman of his own class, Lady Lancing felt she would have her revenge on that little upstart Bettina Newton.

When Michael would have honoured her by seating her next to himself, she refused with a coy titter, declaring that she was sure he would much rather sit next to Lady Alice.

Thus Michael found himself sitting beside Alice whether he liked it or not.

"Miss Newton," he said quickly, "as you are our hostess, will you honour me by sitting on my other side?"

Bettina murmured something and took the seat. In fact she had no choice, since Michael was gripping her wrist with a firmness of which only she was aware.

Michael could feel Alice sitting as close to him as she possibly could. When he spoke to Bettina he could feel Alice's anger reaching him in waves.

'This is ridiculous,' he thought.

He therefore said aloud to the Major,

"It is so good of you to have us for luncheon, Major. Afterwards we must have our discussion. I know you have a great deal to tell me about how the work is proceeding."

"But surely you don't need to supervise every detail yourself," Alice said. "Why, I am certain that the Major is hoping you will return to London and leave him to carry on undisturbed."

"Not at all," the Major said heartily. "I prefer a client who takes a close interest."

"And I am going to stay here until I have achieved my object," Michael stated firmly. "There is no question of me altering my mind."

For a moment there was a rather uncomfortable silence.

As if he was aware of the tension, the Major began to talk about his time as a soldier, when he had discovered that many countries boasted flowers which could heal human beings.

"I hope you are writing a book about it?" Michael enquired.

"I have made a start," the Major replied. "But when I try to concentrate there is always a knock on the door and someone wants my help. By the time I return to my desk I find it difficult to remember what I had intended to say."

"You should allocate set hours for those who seek your help," Michael suggested. "It is how doctors work and this book of yours is going to be important.

"As soon as the castle is finished I shall invite you to stay, Major. You will be locked in one of the rooms at the very top and no one will disturb you."

"I will remind you of that one day soon," the Major answered smiling.

Alice gave a cry.

"You are not to encourage him to stay down here for ever. He is wanted in London."

She added slyly,

"Or perhaps, if he will not come to London, then London must come to him."

At this threat Michael paled. He was being hunted with more determination than he had realised.

He glanced sideways at Bettina who, he felt, was his only protection.

He found her looking at him and was aware again of her blue eyes and sweet face.

He thought she was undoubtedly the prettiest girl he had seen for a long time. In fact he could not remember anyone more beautiful.

There was something about her which was different from all the girls he had met and danced with in London.

He could not put it into words, yet he knew it instinctively. She was unique and in every way different from Alice.

'How is it possible?' he asked himself. 'She is a country girl, who I am quite certain has never been to London or enjoyed the gaiety and excitement of 'coming out' as a *debutante*. Yet, in some extraordinary way, I feel she knows more about life than Alice and is certainly a lot more intelligent.'

Then he told himself he was being ridiculous. It was quite impossible to compare the two women.

And yet the thought lingered.

Lady Lancing felt that the table had lasted long enough without the benefit of her observations.

"What a cosy, delightful, little feast," she gushed. "And so much more to your taste, Miss Newton, I feel sure, than the banquet at the castle."

Seeing Alice register surprise, she swept on,

"Oh, my dear Lady Alice, did nobody tell you? Lord Danesbury gave a great feast at the castle and Miss Newton acted as his hostess."

Alice gave an audible hiss.

Michael groaned inwardly.

Bettina held her breath.

"It was such a delightful occasion," Lady Lancing resumed, apparently oblivious but actually taking in every detail. "Of course Miss Newton is not experienced, but we all felt she did very well. Very well indeed."

"Miss Newton was in every way what a hostess should be," Michael declared firmly. "I could not have asked for better."

Alice did not hiss again, but her silence was more ominous than words.

This time it was Win who began to talk determinedly, asking the Major questions about plants and displaying a knowledge of the subject that Michael had not known him to possess.

When he flagged Michael took over, discussing the castle grounds, so that when the meal was finally finished,

Alice was able to draw Michael outside to the garden and say,

"You have had your talk with the Major, so now you can return to the castle with me and show me my bedroom."

Inwardly Michael groaned to discover that she had not relinquished this idea.

"You will need to return to London," he suggested hopefully, "and you should leave now."

Alice gave a merry peal of laughter.

"Nonsense, darling, I am not going. I came to help you and from what I have seen already, you *do* need my help."

"Alice, it would ruin your reputation to stay alone with me at the castle."

There was silence for a moment. Then Alice responded archly,

"It would hardly matter if we were engaged publicly instead of privately."

"We are not engaged. I am sorry to be blunt, but you must understand once and for all, *we are not engaged.*"

There was more silence before Alice replied,

"You know that Papa and all of London expect us to marry each other."

"Then they will learn that they are wrong," he retorted bluntly.

She laid her hand on his arm, trying to draw even nearer to him.

"You do not mean that, I love you and you love me. Let's return to the castle and tonight we will have a long talk."

Michael drew a sharp breath,

"What you suggest is impossible. I advise you to go

back to London immediately before anyone hears of such outrageous behaviour. It is only too easy to become the talk of Mayfair and then the gossip will reach the Queen's ear."

"Oh, the Queen desires our marriage as much as anyone else," Alice replied blithely. "Oh, darling, let's not fight. You need a Mistress for your wonderful castle. I will turn it into a showpiece for you."

Michael felt his head whirl. Was there any way to get through to her? But of course, she was obeying her parents' dictates. He was fighting not only Alice, but a vast unseen army behind her, at the head of which was the Prince of Wales and behind him, his formidable mother, Queen Victoria.

"You are returning to London, right now," he ordered firmly. "I will escort you to your carriage."

But Alice still held one more card to play. As Michael took her hand, meaning to draw it firmly through his arm, she gave a little moan, murmuring,

"Forgive me, I feel so strange."

The next moment she had fainted dead away against him. Michael found himself holding her inert body, looking around desperately for someone to assist him.

Help came in the blessed appearance of Bettina. Taking in the situation at a glance, she hurried up to them and forcibly took the burden of Alice's body from him onto herself.

"Be so kind as to fetch Miss Paxton to aid me," she said.

"Of course. Are you sure you can manage?"

"Oh, I am as strong as a donkey," she assured him cheerfully. "And I can assure you, Lady Alice will wish to be tended only by members of her own sex."

Luckily Katherine appeared at that moment and the

two of them helped Alice into the house, where they laid her down on the sofa.

Bettina knelt down by her head and Katherine, who had formed a tolerably good idea of the situation, stood between the sofa and Michael.

Alice stirred and gave a little moan.

"Michael – "

"Do not move, Lady Alice," Bettina said solicitously. "You are quite safe and Lord Danesbury is just going to fetch you a glass of fresh spring water."

"Yes, indeed," Michael agreed and hastened away.

Thwarted, Alice was forced to lie back and be patient. When Michael returned with the glass he handed it to Katherine, who handed it to Bettina, who handed it in turn to Alice.

Alice watched this byplay with cold, narrow eyes.

"I am not well," she whispered. "I cannot face the journey back to London."

Michael tensed, sensing danger, but Bettina spoke calmly.

"Of course you cannot, but never fear. You can remain in this house until you are well. I will prepare your own bedroom."

"You are too kind," Alice replied desperately, "but I would not dream of depriving you. Lord Danesbury must take me to the castle – "

"Indeed no!" Bettina said earnestly. "Never fear, you shall not be asked to risk your reputation in such a way. You will stay here and Lord Danesbury will return to his castle. Being a great gentleman, he will undertake not to visit you even once until you return home. You *will* do that, won't you, my Lord."

"My word on it," Michael concurred, looking at her

with admiration.

"I would not turn you out of your own home," Alice pleaded to Michael, beginning to become desperate. "It is such a big place, you could still be there – "

"That would be most inadvisable," Bettina asserted firmly. "In fact, it might even be better if Lord Danesbury visited your parents in London to tell them where you are.

"Then everyone would know that you are here and he in London and so there would be no way he could possibly have compromised you. Will that not be a good idea?"

She beamed at Alice, who stared back, glassy-eyed as she realised that she had met her match.

Just when it seemed that the situation could not possibly become more fraught, Lady Lancing reappeared, looking this way and that to detect anything that might have escaped her.

"My dear Lady Alice," she enquired, sweeping forward, "are you ill? I have heard such alarming reports."

Bettina's eyes gleamed. She knew the way her enemy's mind worked and she knew how she could turn it to her advantage.

"We were just arranging for Lady Alice to remain here as the guest of my father and myself until she has fully recovered," she volunteered.

Exactly as she had expected, Lady Lancing sat on this idea.

"How kind, my dear Miss Newton, but I fear your little home is not quite what Lady Alice is used to." She smiled at Alice. "You will of course come to stay with me, dear Lady Alice."

Agreeable visions of having an Earl's daughter as her guest, of visits from Lord and Lady Randall, and endless chances to boast to her cronies, danced before Lady Lancing's eyes, making her add,

"In fact I hope I can tempt you to stay for a really *long* visit."

Alice had endured as much as she could stand. Her temper was rising and she realised that if she was forced to listen to any more of these provincials she would explode.

She struggled to her feet.

"You are very kind," she managed to say, "but I believe I am now well enough to travel."

"I will call your coachman to the door immediately," Michael offered. "And he will take you straight back to London."

He vanished hastily, giving thanks for Bettina's quick wits.

He instructed Alice's coachman to be ready to depart at once for London and then walked back inside to announce,

"Your coach is ready, Lady Alice."

Alice made one last try.

"If I might have one moment alone with you – ?"

"I would not dream of tiring you," he replied promptly.

Courtesy demanded that he proffer her his arm as she left the house, but Bettina and Katherine stuck close to them, giving Alice no chance to play any more of her tricks.

Soon she was aboard the carriage and it was pulling away. She flung a reproachful look back at Michael, who stood, his hand on Bettina's shoulder, watching her go.

"You did it," he murmured.

"We did it," she said.

Suddenly he turned, making her turn as well, so that he could hold her by both shoulders.

"No, *you* did it," he said. "I could not have managed without you. *You were wonderful.*"

Without warning he was overtaken by emotion. He

tightened his hands on her shoulders and swept her into his arms. The next moment his lips were on hers in an exuberant kiss.

It was so swift that Bettina was taken utterly by surprise. For a moment she could not react and when a glimpse of sanity returned, she realised that there was nothing she could do.

Most likely Alice was still close enough to see them and if she struggled, or boxed his ears like the last time, Alice would see that too and be even more suspicious than she was already.

So she stayed still in his arms, intending to let him feel how frozen she was. But she could not stay frozen. An insidious warmth was creeping over her and with it a sweetness that made her head spin.

Now she knew how badly she had wanted to be kissed by him. In fact, she had secretly wanted just this, ever since that first time by the river.

She knew that he was not for her. She had tried to be sensible, fighting off her growing love for him and then refusing to acknowledge it.

But with this impulsive act he had brought her completely under his spell. She was lost, hopelessly in love, with no chance of hiding it from herself. Or perhaps even from him.

It was really not fair for him to destroy her good resolutions like this. And why? To make a point to Lady Alice? What did he care for her feelings?

At the thought that he was simply making use of her, her temper began to rise. Now she raised her hands and pressed them against him gently but firmly.

"Let me go," she muttered.

He released her lips.

"Bettina, I am sorry, I didn't mean – "

"I know exactly what you meant," she cried furiously. "This is unpardonable. Release me this instant."

"Don't be angry with me – "

"Sir, you are not behaving like a gentleman and if you do not let me go at once, I shall box your ears so hard that your head will not stop spinning for a week."

Suddenly he seemed to understand her.

"Oh, Heavens, I am sorry – I forgot – "

He released her. Bettina took a swift look round and was glad to see that Alice's carriage had vanished and nobody was in the road.

"Forgot what?" she seethed.

"Him! Your fiancé. I just cannot seem to remember him, but of course if you are in love with him – "

"Oh, go away!" she cried and rushed back into the house.

CHAPTER EIGHT

Michael and Win dined alone that evening. Both were feeling drained and tired. They spoke little over the food and then took their port into the library.

"Who would have believed it?" Win mused. "Mind you, even I have to admit that she is incredibly beautiful."

"Incredibly," Michael murmured.

"Such eyes!"

"Wonderful eyes," Michael echoed.

"You could not be blamed if – mind you, it was a shock when I looked out of the window and saw you holding her."

Michael tensed and looked at him sharply.

"You saw that?"

"I saw everything, old fellow. For a moment I thought you were a gonner, but Miss Newton came to your rescue. Never known a woman with such presence of mind. Of course, Katherine helped, but it was Miss Newton who saved the day."

Michael allowed himself to relax.

"You – saw Alice faint?" he asked carefully.

"Yes, of course. What did you think I meant?"

"Nothing, nothing," he said hastily. "I was just being sure."

To change the subject, he said,

"You called Miss Paxton 'Katherine'."

Win jumped as though someone had pinched him.

"Did I? I meant Miss Paxton of course."

"Not playing fast and loose, are you, Win? She *is* the Vicar's daughter."

"Hang that! Do you think it's just respect for her father that makes me – I mean – she is the finest, most wonderful – I'm going to bed!"

He drained his port and hurried out of the library, leaving Michael a prey to astonishment.

So old Win had fallen at last, not for a dazzling beauty or an heiress, but for a girl with nothing to recommend her but a pair of fine eyes and a gentle, determined character.

Just what Win needed, really!

But while he enjoyed these thoughts, Michael recognised that he was simply putting off other thoughts – about himself and Bettina.

They were troubled, a mysterious combination of uneasiness and delight.

He remembered the warmth of the sun and the touch of Bettina's lips against his.

'I should have tried harder to keep away from her,' he reflected. 'But I could not help myself.'

He poured himself another glass of port as his meditation took a darker turn.

'What's the use? She doesn't want me. How can I allow myself fall in love with a girl who is always angry with me and threatening me with violence? Box my ears, indeed!'

He sighed as something else occurred to him.

'Of course, if she really *is* engaged, she has every reason to be angry with me. But *is* she?'

He had begun to disbelieve in the mysterious fiancé, thinking him no more than a ruse to keep himself at a distance. But Bettina's rage with him today had made him think again.

He probably existed. And would soon arrive to sweep her away.

Michael discovered that he would mind this very much indeed.

'Why do these strange things always happen to me?' he mused.

But even as he asked the question, he knew the answer. He was seeing strange things because he himself was strange.

Just as no one else he had ever met had possessed a castle like his, he would continue to be strange and different when it was finished and people would still be astounded at what he had achieved.

'This is a great task,' he told himself. 'Suddenly I have become aware of issues I never even thought about – history – something I rarely bothered with, at least not in relation to myself.

'But now I see the great sweep of centuries, all seeming to converge on this castle, of which I am the trustee as much as the owner. Father to son for generations and in my turn I shall pass it on to my son, and after me, my family will continue the legacy.'

In this new mood the thought of having a son pleased him. Two or three sons, perhaps, and daughters too. And a wife –

But what kind of a wife?

Who, among the women he knew, would be content to live in the country and love the castle as he did?

Not Alice or anyone of her ilk. He felt more distant from Society females now than ever before.

Not a fashionable lady, then. A girl with her roots in the country, who loved the world he loved. A girl with golden hair and shining eyes and a quiet, gentle manner.

But not an insipid girl. She must have spirit and courage enough to stand up to him. He would rather enjoy her giving him as good as she received, as long as she loved him.

Abruptly he rose and walked upstairs to bed. He was not ready to think any further on this subject. It was beginning to alarm him.

*

Michael was up early next morning and hurried down to breakfast.

He was just enjoying the fish which Mrs. Brooks had cooked for him, when the post arrived.

"I will open it while I finish breakfast," Michael said.

There were six letters. Most looked like bills, but on one the handwriting was familiar.

"Peter," he exclaimed.

He meant his friend Sir Peter Heston, who had been one of the first to warn him, several weeks earlier, that he was expected to propose marriage to Alice.

He lived at the centre of Society and always knew the latest gossip.

Perhaps now, Michael thought, he had written to say that his disappearance had been successful.

'Except that I saw Alice only yesterday,' he thought. 'So I have not been as successful as all that. He is probably warning me that she is on her way here."

But the news was much, much worse than that.

Just for a moment he felt as if the writing on the letter was swimming in front of his eyes.

It said,

"*Dear Michael,*

I hear from your servants that you are working very hard in the country and have no intention, as far as they know, of returning to London. I therefore hope I am not bringing you bad news.

But the fact is that you are by no means out of danger.

Alice's father, has, for the moment, stopped abusing your name every time he visits his club.

I thought perhaps he had given up the chase and was looking elsewhere for his son-in-law.

Unfortunately I heard yesterday that he has been to see the Queen and he asked to see her privately. It is certain that he was going to speak to Her Majesty about you.

So perhaps the most sensible thing you can do is to leave immediately for the Continent.

You will doubtless find much to entertain you in Paris or Italy.

If you stay away for a month or so the whole matter will have blown over, or the girl will have found other prey.

The best of luck, old man, and I only hope that you will be able to escape. But get away fast, as once Her Majesty gives an order she expects it to be carried out immediately.

Send me a letter from the Continent, giving me your address. I might easily find myself joining you!

With all blessings for the future,

Yours,

Peter."

PS: The Prince of Wales has been asking after you as well.

Michael read the letter through once and then again.

It seemed to him that he was caught in a trap, from

which it was impossible to escape.

If he fled abroad, as his friend had suggested, he knew he would be longing, every moment, to be back at the castle.

What was more, he was quite certain that the works could not be completed as he wanted, unless he was present to supervise every detail.

'What *can* I do? What the hell can I do?' he asked himself. 'Without me, everything will slip back and I will lose everything I have gained.'

He strode to the open window feeling as if he needed fresh air.

'Oh, help me God, what *can* I do?'

He looked up to the sky, glorious with the early morning sun.

And he remembered the sun of yesterday, which had turned Bettina's hair to gold.

He recalled the colour had seemed to glint at him when his lips touched hers.

It was a moment of wonder and glory – the glory he was striving to create at the castle when restored to its original splendour and the garden was as beautiful as the Major's.

And then, almost as if the answer came from Heaven itself, he understood how he could prevent the Queen or anyone else, from forcing him to marry Alice.

'It's impossible!' he said to himself. 'Crazy! Absurd. She will box my ears for even daring to suggest it!'

But it was indeed a way to save the castle and to save himself.

He was not quite certain which was the most important.

But whatever the answer, there was no alternative.

It was this or nothing.

After Alice's visit he felt even less desire to marry her than before.

In her own way she had frightened him so much that he was ashamed of himself for feeling as he did.

But that left only the inspiration that had just come to him, an idea so extraordinary that he could almost laugh at himself for thinking of it.

He returned to his breakfast without tasting what he was eating or drinking. Just as he was finishing, Brooks came in to say that the man who was working on the roof wished to speak to him.

Michael hurried out.

"What is the trouble, Cooper?" he asked.

"I think your Lordship should climb up and look at what we're doing," he answered. "I'm sure that we should make the roof a little stronger than we planned. If the wind was strong it might easily blow away or damage the top of the castle."

Michael followed him immediately and when they reached the turret, he found that he was quite right.

"As it is," Cooper pointed out, "the winter winds would tear it to pieces."

"They certainly would," Michael said. "I should have thought of it before. The roof looks very attractive but it is too light. Double its strength and it should be strong enough to withstand any gale, however violent."

As he walked down the stairs he was thinking that the gale that was facing *him* at the moment could not be pushed aside so easily.

'Suppose if I had not been here to make the decision?' he mused. 'What would they have done? That settles it. I cannot leave. It will have to be the other way.'

*

At the other end of the village the Major had risen in a bad temper.

If there was one thing he found incredibly boring it was to be forced to attend the extremely tiresome meetings called by the Lord Lieutenant every month.

He insisted on everyone of any importance in the locality attending. There was usually nothing vital to discuss but it made the Lord Lieutenant feel that he mattered to the County.

"I have to travel six miles to his house," the Major complained to Bettina over breakfast. "Then spend two hours talking a lot of nonsense about nothing."

"It is only once a month," Bettina said. "And you have to attend because you are so important."

"Fiddlesticks!" the Major retorted sharply. "I have to go so that the old fool can feel important. Plus, of course, that dreadful woman he married. It was bad enough having her gatecrash our lunch yesterday without having to listen to her again today."

"She will probably fire off a few barbed remarks about me," Bettina observed.

"Why should she?"

"My first crime was Lord Danesbury asking me to be hostess. My second was – well, just about everything that happened yesterday."

"Pooh! Load of nonsense! Why do women make so much of nothing?"

"I cannot imagine," Bettina replied in a voice that gave nothing away.

"I should really spend today working on our garden," the Major remarked, apparently oblivious to the cloud that seemed to have settled over his daughter. "After you and the Earl took Lady Alice clodhopping all over it!"

Bettina managed a smile.

"Papa, Lady Alice is a Society lady. She does not clodhop!"

"They do when they are stupid and ignorant and don't know a flower from a weed. What were the two of you thinking about to allow her to stamp all over everything?"

"Well, if you will plant your flowers so close to each other, it's very difficult not to stand on them. Another cup of tea, Papa?"

He held out his cup, not seeming to notice how quickly she had changed the subject.

In fact, she thought sadly, he never noticed how she was feeling these days. He had always been a most affectionate father, but now his concern for the castle gardens seemed to have overtaken him so completely that he had no attention to spare for her.

When at last Bettina waved her father off, she stood wondering whether to go back inside and continue with her work, or to wander through the garden.

At last she turned her steps towards the garden.

Here she could be alone and indulge her thoughts. But she had been indulging them ever since the party broke up the day before, and she was no nearer knowing what she truly thought and felt.

Bettina had been angry with Michael for kissing her, and yet in her heart she had known that there was something about his kiss that could not make her angry, but made her feel something very different from anger.

It had been so different from that other kiss on the first day. Then he had stolen his pleasure almost casually. She could have been anyone and she had felt insulted.

But the second kiss had been gentle and tender, with a passion and sweetness that she would remember all her life.

For a moment she could have sworn that he was thinking of nothing but her.

It was she who had broken the spell by losing her temper, assuming that he was merely making use of her.

But suppose he had not been doing so? Suppose he had really meant it?

She chided herself for her foolishness.

Of course it could come to nothing. Between an Earl and an Army Major's daughter there could never be any thought of marriage.

Her anger of the day before had melted away. Now she acquitted him of trifling with her. He had been overpowered by the magic of the moment – just as she had.

She could never marry him, but she would always love him and cherish his kiss in her heart forever.

At that moment, to her surprise, she detected the clatter of horse's hooves coming down the road.

At first she did not believe that she was really seeing Michael. It seemed as though she must have conjured him up from her thoughts and from her heart.

He saw her and turned his horse into the garden, trotting right up to her before he dismounted.

The sight of him made her want to smile with joy, although she tried not to let him see. The feeling for him that had grown within her must be hidden – from him most of all.

"Good morning," she said, trying to sound cheerful and normal. "If you want to see Papa, I am afraid he has just left and will not return until this evening."

"Actually," Michael replied, "I came to see you on a rather important matter. Can we go inside and talk privately?"

"Of course," she agreed, puzzled by his manner.

He tied his horse to a tree and followed her into the

drawing room. It was a delightful room at the side of the house overlooking the river.

The sunshine was making the flowers in the garden almost too vivid to be real. Beyond the river shone as it passed swiftly along in front of the trees on the other side.

"The view from here is marvellous," he started, going to the window.

Bettina thought that this was a strange remark to make. He had said he wanted to speak to her on an important matter, but now he was making idle comments about the view.

It did not occur to her that he was playing for time, trying to gather courage to say what was really on his mind.

"I feel so too. But of course, until Papa arrived, it was rather barren and uninteresting. He made it marvellous just as he will do with your garden."

"If he is lucky enough to have the time to complete it," Michael said.

"What are you saying? You sound as if something has gone wrong."

"Yes, something *has* gone wrong," he replied. "So I have come here to ask you to help me. No, don't speak!"

He held up his hand to forestall anything she might say. Bettina noticed how pale he was.

"I know what you are going to say," he added desperately.

"Do you?"

"I begged for your help yesterday and then abused your hospitality. My behaviour was atrocious, unforgivable. And yet I am asking you to forgive me, because nobody in the world can save me except you."

Something in his manner, a new gravity that she had not seen before, made her pause and stare at him. Now she realised that he was full of tension.

Impulsively she stretched out her hand.

"Nothing is as bad as it seems at first," she said. "If anything has gone wrong, you know we will do our best to help you."

"We?"

"Papa and me."

"No, just you. Nobody else can do anything for me."

It had occurred to Bettina that perhaps he was running out of money, but then he would not be speaking to her. He must know that she had no money.

Gathering her courage she took both his hands and drew him towards the sofa. They sat down together.

"Tell me everything," she coaxed.

His silence was frightening her. What could be so bad that he could not speak?

Eventually he said,

"I can only tell you the truth and beg you on my knees to help me. Otherwise, if you will not do so, my only alternative is to leave England immediately."

"Leave England!" Bettina exclaimed. "I don't understand, what has happened?"

To her surprise he looked away from her, as though in confusion.

Impulsively Bettina moved a little nearer to him on the sofa.

"Tell me," she urged.

Instead of speaking, he took the letter out of his pocket and showed it to her. As Bettina read Sir Peter's words, Michael saw a puzzled look spread over her face.

Of course, he thought, she had never encountered this kind of calculated scheming and barely understood the implications when she met it now.

It was just one more quality that made her so enchanting.

Bettina read the letter through twice. Her heart was beating hard.

"I told you about Alice yesterday," Michael began. "I liked her well enough at the start, although I was never in love with her. We danced together often at parties. Then one day she said people were talking about us. They had noted how often we danced and that we talked too long in the garden. So, according to her, I had compromised her and therefore we must marry."

Bettina gave an exclamation of surprise.

"Why should you marry her just because you have danced with her?" she asked.

"There is no reason, of course, except her father's ambition."

"I do not understand that kind of ambition," Bettina replied simply. "Surely what matters is that you marry someone you love?"

"Exactly," he agreed. "That is what I desire and I certainly do not wish to marry Alice who, in any case, will never love the castle as I do. She will view it as a beautiful backdrop for herself and then want to return to London as soon as possible."

"And she will care nothing for the people here, who need you so much," Bettina admitted. "But surely, after what happened yesterday, she must understand that you will never propose to her."

"I think she does understand it. That is why she is resorting to coercion," Michael added bitterly. "I told you yesterday that her father has the Queen's ear."

"Yes, but I could hardly believe that you could actually

be commanded to marry her by the Queen – it's incredible – can that sort of thing really happen?"

"It has happened several times in the last few months and now it's happening to me. My only alternative is to go abroad."

"Oh, no, you must not," she said quickly. "You are so needed here. All the good work will be undone if you leave."

"That is what I think too," Michael told her. "My only hope is to say I am engaged or, better still, already married."

He spoke so quietly it was hard for her to hear his words.

Bettina, staring at him, did not understand.

At last she asked, cautiously,

"How is that possible?"

There was silence for a moment before Michael answered,

"That, my dear Bettina, is what I am asking you."

He realised as he spoke, how outrageous she would think his idea was when she had heard it.

He saw the astonishment in her eyes.

Then she said in a strange voice,

"What are you saying? I – do not understand."

"When the Queen's Messenger arrives, I must be able to tell him that I am already married."

Bettina stared at him. Suddenly the air seemed to be singing about her ears.

"Do you mean – that you want me to – ?"

"To pretend to be my wife," Michael said. "Now I think of it, an engagement will not be enough to make them give up. They must think I am actually married and thus beyond their reach."

"But will it work? Can it actually be that simple? Will

122

they demand details?"

"We might have to say where we were married and who performed the ceremony, but I think if you were kind enough to play the part, we could say that we were married in the North of England where I have some relatives."

Bettina was gazing at him as he resumed,

"We will have to invent some reason for our marriage to be kept a secret for the moment. You might have a relative who has died recently and you would therefore be in mourning for at least six months."

"That might be one way," she agreed slowly. "Or perhaps I could conjure up a relative of my own in the North of England where they are not likely to make enquiries. In fact it might have to be as far away as Scotland."

He gripped her hands.

"I know I am asking a great deal of you, but my dear Bettina, I am desperate."

Bettina's head shot up. Her eyes were flashing with determination.

"You must not leave," she repeated. "Anything would be better. The locals need you so much. You are their only hope."

"And you are *my* only hope," he said fervently. "Without your help I must go abroad. I absolutely refuse to be forced into marriage against my will!"

He spoke so violently that Bettina could only sympathise with him.

In a soft voice she said,

"I will do whatever you want me to do."

CHAPTER NINE

For a moment, after Bettina had spoken, there was complete silence.

Then Michael asked, in a voice which did not sound like his own,

"Do you really mean that?"

"Of course I mean it," Bettina replied sincerely. "How could I not do anything you ask, when you are being so good to us all?"

"All?"

"You have given us all such hope. Believe me, any one of us would do anything for you."

"But I am not asking any of the others," he said quietly. "Only you."

"And I will help you, of course I will," she responded in a voice whose soft fervour seemed to touch his heart.

Michael stared at her. It was on the tip of his tongue to ask her why she was doing this? Was it *only* for the sake of the people of the neighbourhood?

Did she care so much for them and nothing for him?

The question danced through his head and out again before he could catch it.

"Tell me how you wish me to behave," Bettina said.

"Perhaps I should not be asking you," he blurted out

suddenly. "I have no right to ask you."

"But of course you have. We must not allow you to be trapped in such a wicked way. You must *not* marry her. What does she care for the castle or the people here?"

"Nothing. You are right. Thank you, but – "

"But?"

"There is one great drawback from your point of view. You have not yet mentioned him, but I know he must be in your thoughts."

"You mean my father?"

"I mean your fiancé."

He caught the briefest flash of bewilderment in her face before she recovered herself. Now he was almost certain that the man did not exist. If only she would admit as much.

He was not quite sure why it was important, but suddenly it was.

He wanted to hear Bettina say with her own lips that she cared for no other man.

"I have already imposed greatly on an engaged woman," he persisted. "Perhaps I ask too much. Surely even the most understanding fiancé in the world would not tolerate this?"

Bettina regarded him with a faint, wry smile.

"My Lord, do you wish me to do this for you or do you not?"

"Of course I do," he declared, determined to press her to an admission, "but if – "

"You need not worry about it."

"I just do not want to harm you with your future husband."

"You may safely leave him to me," she informed him.

Her eyes met his, challenging, daring him to contradict her.

What a woman!

Emboldened, he tried again.

"Do you know, you have never told me his name?"

"How can his name possibly concern you?"

"Never mind," he said cheerfully. "I will find out when he arrives to marry you."

They looked at each other, each understanding the other perfectly and neither willing to admit it.

"One more word," she threatened, "and I will push you out of that door!"

"With your left hook?"

"Right," she said firmly.

"Right. How could I have forgotten, after having felt it?"

"My Lord, I give you fair warning – "

"Not another word, I promise you. I would not offend you for the world. You are my saviour, and – and I will never forget your kindness."

Michael spoke the last words slowly, holding her hands.

There was a silence which for the moment neither of them could break. At the same time they both seemed to become aware that their hands were still clasped – and hastily separated.

"We need to be prepared for anything," Michael said. "If you agree, I think we should now go back to the castle and wait there to see who arrives."

"But surely, they won't be in such a hurry?"

"The Queen's command is the Queen's command," he answered, "and anything she orders needs to be carried out immediately."

He looked up at the clock on the mantelpiece and said,

"It is now almost ten o'clock. If anyone is coming today, he will arrive just before luncheon and expect to be given a good meal. Then he will leave congratulating not me, but himself on having carried out the Queen's orders."

Michael spoke bitterly.

Bettina guessed at how much all this had upset him.

He was not only embarrassed at what he had asked of her, but felt ashamed to find himself in such an intolerable predicament.

She rose and said,

"I will go upstairs and dress in my best clothes, if – if you will wait for me."

The words seemed to come from her lips rather jerkily.

Michael too felt awkward.

There was so much happening that neither of them could articulate.

He almost forced himself to say,

"Thank you. You know I find it difficult to tell you how grateful I am."

"Do not talk about it," Bettina replied quickly. "I will change quickly and we can be on our way to the castle."

"This is madness," he cried suddenly. "It cannot possibly work."

"It *must* work," Bettina asserted. "We cannot lose you."

"We – again?" Michael could not resist asking.

Bettina coloured a little.

"I am not just doing this for you, but for everyone. If I didn't help you I would feel that I was letting my friends and neighbours down."

"Of course I understand that," he said quietly.

Without waiting for him to reply, she disappeared.

Michael was left staring at the door, wishing he knew what was really going through her mind.

'A lot of women,' he thought, 'would find the plan degrading. She can rise above it for the sake of others. But what does she want for herself?'

He gave a deep sigh, closing his eyes as he realised that the tension was lifting from his shoulders. Suddenly he was so full of relief that he wanted to shout with joy.

Bettina was on his side. Bettina would be fighting for him. With such an ally, he could not possibly lose.

He tried to calm himself by fetching his horse from the garden, bringing the gig from the stables, and tying his horse behind it. Then he walked back into the house to wait for Bettina.

He hoped she would not be too long. Pacing up and down, he found that his worries began to crowd in on him again.

Then he heard the door open behind him and he turned swiftly. What he saw made him grow very still.

Bettina was dressed with an elegance he had seen in her only once before – on the night of the dinner party. Then she had been in evening dress. Now she was dressed for the day and she was smart and exquisite.

She might have been going to a big luncheon party in Mayfair. Her gown was pink, matching the roses on her hat.

For a moment Michael just stared at her before asking her,

"How can you look so magnificent and so lovely?

Bettina laughed.

"It is most impolite of you to be so surprised."

"No, I didn't mean – " he stopped, aware that he was stammering like a schoolboy. He had a horrible feeling that

128

he was also going red.

Bettina did not feel it necessary to tell him that she had obtained this dress by exchanging it with the black and gold one she had worn for the dinner. Mrs. Tandy had discovered another customer for the evening gown and had been willing to take it back.

Bettina had been sad to part with the gown which had first made Michael look at her with astonishment and admiration, but she knew she would never wear it again. In the end, the lure of some beautiful day dresses had proved too much.

Now, when she saw the same astonishment and admiration in his eyes again, she was glad she had made the exchange.

"I thought I should look as smart as possible," she explained. "Then, if the Queen's Messenger arrives before luncheon, we can say that we are just going out to a party being given in our honour."

"That's excellent. Go on."

"We must apologise but say we are unable to ask him in for a meal. In fact we can only invite him in for a glass of champagne to drink our good health."

She smiled as she added,

"Next we suggest he returns to London, because we are going to be the guests of the Lord Lieutenant. If, later on, he enquires whether the Lord Lieutenant actually gave a party on this day, he will learn that he did."

The way she spoke made Michael laugh.

"What a wonderful little strategist you are. I can tell you are a daughter of a soldier."

"Thank you, kind sir, but I think you really mean a tactician."

"Do I?"

"I am not a soldier's daughter for nothing. You employ strategy while the enemy is out of sight and tactics when he appears. This enemy is almost upon us!"

"But the wretched messenger isn't the real enemy. There are several of them and they are all in London."

"True," she conceded. "You are quite right."

"But you are right too," he hurried to say. "You seem very much in command of what you are doing, which relieves my mind, because I am so much in your hands."

"Do not worry about it. We will defeat them."

Suddenly he cried out,

"You are magnificent. You look exactly as I should ask my wife to look if we were going to a Society occasion."

She laughed.

"You are very kind, but I am sure I could never pass muster in fashionable salons."

'I would like to take her into Society,' he thought. 'She is beautiful enough to grace any drawing room, while her freshness and natural manners make her a delight after the artificial world I am accustomed to.'

But he did not feel he could say this to her while he had placed her in such a delicate position, so he merely said,

"Let us go quickly now."

She took the arm he offered and they walked out together to the waiting gig.

Bettina felt as though she was travelling in a dream. Everything that was happening to her was impossible and yet it was really happening.

So many impossibilities had occurred since Michael had arrived. Suddenly the world had become so beautiful, full of hope and promise.

It was hard to remember that basically it was all an illusion. One day he would leave, if not for good then for a few months to resume his life in London.

When he had told her his problem, her first horrified thought was that he must not go. She had covered her dismay by talking about the locality and how much it needed him.

But the truth, which had shocked her almost to dumbness, was that she could not bear the thought of life without him nearby. How empty everything would be. How wretched and lonely!

How could she ever be happy again?

One day it would happen and she would be condemned to eternal loneliness. He would find a bride from Society, somebody very different from Alice and he would bring her to the castle. And she, Bettina, would have to endure seeing them together.

She gave herself a little shake. She had promised to help him and if she was to keep her word she must think only of his needs, not of herself.

So she pushed gloomy thoughts aside to concentrate on the matter in hand.

There would be time enough to be unhappy later.

"Oh, Heavens!"

The softly vehement exclamation from beside her made her turn to see Michael clutching his head, an expression of horror on his face.

"What is it?" she asked anxiously. "Are you ill?"

"No, but I have just thought of something that I should have remembered sooner."

"What? For goodness sake, tell me!"

"Alice was here yesterday. She met you. If they question her, she will say that nobody mentioned anything about our being married."

At the thought Michael felt his whole body tighten.

For a moment he was almost panic-stricken.

It was all hopeless. The messenger would not believe he had married Bettina.

"It's no use," he groaned. "I am trapped."

"Oh, no, you are not!" Bettina retorted in a firm voice. "Not if I have anything to do with it."

Michael gazed at her.

"Alice returned to London late last night, didn't she?" Bettina asked.

"Yes."

"That letter you received this morning, when was it sent?"

"It must have been posted yesterday."

"While she was still here?"

"Yes," he said, beginning to catch her drift.

"Is it likely that the messenger would visit her this morning before leaving?"

"I suppose he might – but probably not."

"Even if he did, would he have asked Alice how she felt about you being commanded to marry her?"

"It would indeed be rather indelicate," Michael agreed.

"Then we still have every hope, do we not?"

"We do, indeed," he said, feeling more cheerful.

"And we are not downhearted?"

"Definitely not."

"Let them throw their regiments at us!" Bettina cried defiantly. "We will repel them!"

Michael laughed.

"What a genius you are at putting new heart into a man! You have missed your vocation. Clearly nature intended you to be a Sergeant Major."

To his surprise some of the pleasure faded from her face. He had meant to compliment her without being heavy-handed, but he recognised that he had said something wrong.

Bettina tried to tell herself not to be foolish. Michael had meant it kindly. It was just that when she knew that she was looking her prettiest for the man she loved, she wanted him to praise her looks, or at least her charm.

What she did not need was to be compared, however flatteringly, to a Sergeant Major.

"We are nearly there," she said brightly. "We should be making further plans."

"What further plans can we make?"

"Well, if we are supposed to be attending a formal function, I think you should change your clothes."

"You are right. I need to look as fine as you do. I don't want to be cast into the shade."

"Now you are making fun of me."

"No, I am just saying how delightful you look."

"That is important too," Bettina answered. "After all with a castle like yours, you will not want an ugly wife."

Michael did not answer as she continued quickly,

"Of course you don't want a wife at all, you only want to stay in your castle and be left in peace."

"Left in peace," he echoed. "How well you understand me! Nobody in London would understand for a moment. That is one reason I was so glad to leave them behind."

"But *have* you managed to leave them behind?" she asked.

"Not yet, but after today I will have done. They will all be defeated."

"I do hope so. But, as my Papa always said, 'never

underestimate your enemy. He can often be far stronger than you expect him to be'."

"Now you are depressing me," Michael protested. "At the same time, I cannot find the words to express how grateful I am to you."

"You must keep all your gratitude until we are successful," Bettina advised him. "And think only of the castle. When it is finished, it is going to be so marvellous that people will come in crowds to admire it."

It passed through Michael's mind he would find that extremely annoying.

But he did not say so.

He wanted peace and quiet, not only to enjoy the castle, but to concentrate on all the other challenges on the estate. They would also keep him busy and interested for a long time.

'How could I possibly,' he asked himself, 'share all this with Alice? She would have no sympathy with it, unlike Bettina who seems to be instinctively in sympathy with me and the castle.'

As if to prove him right, Bettina said,

"Now you must not worry! I am praying that everything will go exactly as you want it to do. But if we let ourselves become nervous, we might make mistakes."

Michael nodded as she carried on,

"We must believe in what we are doing and try to convince ourselves that what we are saying is the real truth."

He grinned.

"You mean that the best way to tell a good lie is to believe it. Is that an Army saying, too?"

Bettina gave a chuckle, but did not reply in words.

"You should write a book," he said. "Your imagination is fertile enough for anything."

"If I ever did write a book, it would end happily," Bettina mused, "and that is what this present drama must do."

As she was speaking they drove in at the front of the castle. To their relief there was no carriage at the door.

"Nobody has arrived yet," Bettina pointed out. "Thank goodness. If the messenger had arrived first, and we had walked in looking like this, he might think it strange that I am dressed in my best, while you are somewhat dilapidated, to put it bluntly."

Michael laughed.

"I was in such a hurry to come to you," he explained, "that I put on the first clothes my valet gave me. He thought I was going to join the workmen as I often do."

Bettina was considering something.

"Do you think I should be stupid?"

Michael stared.

"I don't think you would know how to be stupid," he said.

"Oh, yes, it's easy if you are a woman. People expect women to be stupid, you see. So if you want to – shall we say – muddle their thoughts a little – you just act vague and everyone assumes it's for real."

Seeing Michael looking at her uncertainly, she gave an inane giggle, gazing at him with wide open eyes.

"That was very effective," he admitted, entranced by the deep blue of her eyes.

"Oh, I can do better than that," she assured him. "If you want, I could sound really half-witted."

She proved her point with another giggle, even vaguer than the first.

"Oh, how *clever* you are," she sighed. "I really don't know how you *intelligent* men put up with us *ridiculous* females. It is so *kind* of you to condescend to us."

"For pity's sake!" Michael said, trying to speak through his laughter. "You are actually a very dangerous woman. I do not think you should be allowed out in public."

Her eyes teased him.

"Has no beautiful lady ever spoken to you like that?"

"Yes, you wretched girl. And now I will never be able to listen to a woman again. I shall always be wondering what she is thinking behind the words."

"I should think you can probably guess what she's thinking," Bettina said outrageously.

"You mean she will be wondering what sort of dunderhead I must be to fall for it. Thank you!"

"Ah, but I feel sure that you do not fall for it, being a man of superior intellect."

"You go too far, my girl."

The laughed out loud together.

"Anyway, just how brainless should I be?" Bettina asked. "Now you have heard my repertoire, should it be Brainless One, or Brainless Two?"

"Brainless One, I think. We don't want to overdo it. Besides, I feel fairly sure that you could not keep Brainless Two going for any length of time. The strain on those sharp wits of yours could be too much even for you."

"Oh, you would be amazed at how stupid I can be when I set my mind to it," she assured him.

"Not really. I think that you are probably an excellent actress and the stage is poorer without you."

They were both laughing as the carriage came to a standstill. One of Michael's grooms came hurrying forward, suppressing his astonishment at the sight of his Lordship driving the shabby gig.

Michael helped Bettina out.

"Here we are," he said. "Into the lion's den. Hold my hand and we will face anything together."

She slipped her hand into his as they ran up the steps.

The first thing they saw was Brooks crossing the hall. Michael hailed him.

"Show Miss Newton into the library and bring her some lemonade while I go upstairs," he ordered.

Brooks did so, leaving Bettina alone for a moment while he fetched the refreshment.

There was a small mirror in a gilt frame on the desk. Bettina glanced into it to check her appearance and felt moderately satisfied.

Suddenly Brooks returned, to announce,

"A gentleman from London to see his Lordship."

Bettina turned round sharply, thankful that Brooks had not addressed her as Miss Newton, which would have been disastrous.

The man who entered was middle aged and good-looking, but exuded a self-important air.

Bettina drew a deep breath, wondering if she could deal with him alone.

But luckily Michael came rushing into the room.

"I heard someone had arrived," he said, "but I did not expect to see you, Lord Stacey."

He held out his hand and the stranger shook it and replied gravely,

"I have come to see you on an important matter. I am here on Her Majesty's orders and I think it would be best if I could please see you alone."

There was a short pause before Michael responded,

"I am delighted to hear from Her Majesty. But first I think you should be introduced to my wife."

As he spoke he turned towards Bettina and held out his hand. She smiled at him and came forward saying as she did so,

"I am longing to know why the Queen sent you here to see my husband."

For a moment Lord Stacey was unable to speak.

Then he said, looking at Michael,

"Did you say that this lady is your *wife*?"

"We were married very quietly," Michael told him. "We are both engaged on restoring this castle, so we decided against a big wedding. It would have been too time consuming."

There was silence.

Both Michael and Bettina became aware that the newcomer was finding it hard to know how to deal with this news.

Finally, with an obvious effort, he said,

"I had no idea that you were married, Danesbury."

"We have kept very quiet about our marriage owing to mourning in my wife's family," Michael told him.

"The Queen will be most surprised to hear this information," Lord Stacey said after a moment. "She will expect me to tell her all the details about when and where the ceremony took place, who were your witnesses, and so on."

Silence.

"Witnesses?" the Michael asked.

"Of course. Even a small private ceremony needs witnesses, otherwise there is no proof that the wedding ever took place. *I am sure you understand me.*"

'He does not believe us,' Bettina thought in horror.

The same thought had evidently occurred to Michael, for he paled visibly. But he was not ready to give up.

"We were married in the North of England, where I have relatives," he said.

"So your relatives were your witnesses?"

"No," he said quickly, knowing that he could not embroil them in this matter.

"Then *who* witnessed your wedding?" Lord Stacey asked, his eyes becoming hard.

"Lord Winton Shriver," Michael asserted decidedly. "We have been good friends for years and he accompanied me on a visit North recently."

This was true. Then, as now, Win's complicated financial affairs had demanded an urgent retreat from London, and the two young men had travelled North to visit two of Michael's aunts.

"So Lord Winton can vouch for your marriage?" Lord Stacey asked.

"Good Heavens, Stacey! Do you doubt me?"

"It is not I that you have to convince, Danesbury, but Her Majesty, who has an infernally suspicious mind when she does not get her own way."

"Well she isn't going to get it this time," Michael replied firmly. "This lady is my wife *and I want no other.*"

A pang coursed through Bettina's heart. He sounded so fervent as he said those words. If only they had been true.

Lord Stacey regarded Bettina coolly.

"And may I ask exactly who this lady is?"

"She is the Countess of Danesbury," Michael declared.

"Of course, but before that?"

"Before that she was Miss Bettina Newton, daughter of Major Newton, lately of Her Majesty's Army, where he saw distinguished service in the East," Michael said in the same firm tone.

"Very well," Lord Stacey said, "if Lord Winton vouches for you that will be that. Is he here?"

"No, he went out early today and will not be back until late."

"How unfortunate!"

On the contrary, Michael was thinking. Win's absence was the most fortunate thing that could have happened. With reasonable luck, he should be able to get a message to him warning him of the questions that Lord Stacey was likely to ask.

He had no doubt that Win would give the right answers. He was a good friend.

But he had to admit to himself that it was all becoming a lot more complicated than he had planned.

And then, the worst nightmare that could possibly happen, did happen.

There was a sound from the hall outside. Footsteps, followed by Win's voice, calling,

"I say, Danesbury, old fellow, are you in there? I must talk to you at once. It's dashed urgent!"

CHAPTER TEN

Michael and Bettina exchanged glances, each frozen with horror at the disaster that would now inevitably engulf them. Everything was lost.

Luckily Lord Stacey did not notice them. His attention was fixed on the door, through which Win strode, his hand clasped in Katherine's.

"Win," Michael called quickly. "What a surprise!"

"Do I understand," Lord Stacey intervened, "that this is Lord Winton Shriver?"

"It is," Michael said. "But perhaps we can delay any further – "

"Lord Winton, I am delighted to meet you," Lord Stacey announced, extending his hand. "I am Lord Stacey, here as the Queen's Messenger."

At the words 'Queen's Messenger' Win stiffened like a deer in a forest, listening for danger and ready to vanish in a moment.

"Er – charmed to meet you," he murmured, shaking hands.

"I am hoping that you can help me," Lord Stacey continued. "I find all this talk of a secret marriage somewhat confusing, but I am assured that you can supply the answer."

Win stared at him before asking hoarsely,

"But how did you – ? Now look here, there's nothing wrong with secret marriages. They are not illegal or anything."

"But a little clandestine, surely?"

"A man may have good reasons for not inviting the world to his wedding," Win declared hotly. "Dashed if I see that it is any business of yours. Come to think of it, big Society weddings are a load of rot. What does a man need except a bride, a preacher and a best man?"

"And witnesses?"

"Well the best man can be a witness, can't he?" Win expostulated. "Never heard of any law against it."

"Ah, yes, a best man. Perhaps we could discuss him."

"Excuse me, we are forgetting our manners," Michael intervened, drawing Katherine forward. "This lady is Miss Katherine Paxton, a great friend of *my wife*." He turned swiftly to Bettina. "Isn't that so, my love?"

"Yes, indeed," Bettina responded.

Win gazed at them blankly.

"Eh? What?"

"So your secret's out at last?" Katherine exclaimed. "I am so glad. It's about time you told the world."

She embraced Bettina, managing to whisper in her ear,

"Have I got it right?"

"Yes," Bettina whispered.

As she stepped away from Katherine, she raised her voice.

"Well, I thought so too, Katherine dear. But I left such a decision to Lord Danesbury. Men are so much better at deciding these matters than we poor females, and of course it is a woman's duty to defer to her husband's superior intellect."

She gazed up at Michael, fluttering her eyelashes in a

theatrical manner that almost ruined his composure.

"Oh, how romantic!" Katherine sighed ecstatically. "Of course, a secret wedding ought not to remain a secret for too long. It really was very naughty of you not to tell Lady Alice yesterday. But I quite see that could have been difficult."

Win gazed at Katherine in admiration as his slower wits began to catch up with hers.

"I say, by Jove!" he said, feeling that these words were safely vague.

"Sorry to have to drag you in, old man," Michael said, clapping Win on the shoulder heartily, "but naturally the marriage has to be proved and since you were my best man, and a witness, you are the obvious person to prove it."

"Of course," Win agreed valiantly. "I will never forget that day."

"Or the way we had to sneak out from The Manor because my aunts had to be kept in the dark, eh?"

With this clue Win's head cleared a little. He recalled the visit to Michael's aunts in Sheffield, a few weeks previously.

Lord Stacey eyed him narrowly.

"Do I understand that you can confirm this wedding, Lord Winton?"

"Of course I can confirm it. I was there."

"And where did it take place?"

"In Sheffield," Win recited.

"When?"

"I say, you ask a dashed load of questions?" Win retorted indignantly. "How do I know? It was several weeks ago and it was raining. I remember that because my boots got wet. Jolly uncomfortable being a best man with wet boots."

Katherine turned away to hide her laughter.

Faced with this united front, Lord Stacey had no choice but to accept defeat.

"Very well," he said at last, "I will convey this intelligence to Her Majesty who, no doubt, will express her own views on the subject, which she will probably convey to you directly."

"I am certain that she will," Michael concurred gravely. "But her felicitations may well miss us, as my wife and I are planning to go abroad for a short honeymoon."

Lord Stacey was obviously overcome by these developments and was anxious to retreat.

Michael showed him to the front door. As soon as he was out of the room the other three gave huge sighs of relief.

Win slipped his arm tightly about Katherine's waist, although whether he was being possessive or holding onto her for safety, Bettina could not be sure.

Michael returned, his eyes gleaming.

"Safe!" he said. "We have won. Miss Newton, you were wonderful."

He took both her hands, laughing into her eyes, and Bettina felt a pang of happiness.

"We were lucky," she said. "If Lord Winton had not joined us just at that moment, saying the right things – "

Then a thought struck her.

"Lord Winton, how did that happen? When that man mentioned a secret marriage, you seemed to know exactly what he was talking about."

"Ah!" Win exclaimed.

"And what was it you wanted to say to me that was so urgent?" Michael asked.

Win took a deep breath, clasped Katherine even more firmly and said,

"I want you to be my best man."

"Glad to, old fellow. So you really have met your fate at last!"

"I certainly have," Win answered, looking happily at Katherine.

"But surely you do not need to go through a secret marriage," Bettina objected.

"Papa is being very unreasonable," Katherine explained. "He says that Winton is not reliable."

"What nonsense!" Michael declared firmly.

"He has refused his consent to our marriage," Katherine sighed, "but as I am of age he cannot prevent us and so we mean to marry without his consent."

"Well done!" Bettina cried at once.

"My darling knows she is getting a very poor bargain," Win said humbly. "I have a tiny estate that my grandmother left me and we intend to live there. I am going to tell my father that it is time I managed without the allowance he gives me."

"He will be so delighted that you are to marry a woman of strength and character that he will probably double it," Michael observed, kissing Katherine on both cheeks.

"But do not marry secretly old fellow," he added. "As Miss Paxton has said, she is of age and nobody can halt the wedding. So, invite your parents and hers. Do not estrange them unnecessarily."

"He is right," Katherine said. "We *should* marry openly."

"Whatever you say, dearest," Win agreed meekly.

"And you can hold the reception at the castle," Michael offered.

Win coughed delicately.

"Very good of you, old fellow," he replied, "but haven't you forgotten something?"

"What?"

"Well – er – difficult situation and all that – er – the fact is – what are you going to do now?"

"Do?"

"When we have this wedding reception at the castle – will Lady Danesbury be presiding?"

"Win, you have windmills in your head. There is no Lady Danesbury."

"But you have just told the world that there is one," Win pointed out. "Once that fellow returns to London and starts talking, I would not be surprised if it is in *The Times* tomorrow."

Michael and Bettina exchanged shocked glances.

"We never thought this far ahead," Bettina whispered.

"So what are you going to do?" Win persisted.

Then a voice came from the doorway.

"I, too, would like an answer to that question."

They all turned to see Major Newton standing there, a frown on his normally amiable face.

The others were too shocked to speak.

The Major advanced into the room and confronted Michael. It occurred to Bettina that she had never seen him quite like this before.

"I have just finished the most interesting – not to say astonishing – conversation with Lord Stacey, as he made his departure," he said. "One of the gardeners happened to address me by name as his carriage was passing, whereupon he stopped the carriage, descended, and proceeded to congratulate me on my daughter's marriage."

"Oh, Papa, what did you say?" Bettina begged.

146

"Nothing that mattered. I made vague noises which he took to be agreement, which is what a soldier is taught to do when confronted with information that he has not had time to assimilate.

"You must allow your father to congratulate you, my dear. Although why you should have married without telling me is beyond my powers of comprehension."

"Oh, Papa, but of course I am not married."

"Then why does Lord Stacey think that you married in Sheffield some weeks ago?"

"I can explain – " she began.

"I think it is for Lord Danesbury to explain," the Major said. "My Lord, I gather that you have persuaded my daughter to pose as your wife in order to extricate yourself from considerable difficulty with Lady Alice.

"What I would like to know is what your intentions are now that you have thoroughly compromised her."

"Papa, he has not – "

"You think not? See what your position is when this news circulates and the village discovers the truth. Do you think Lady Lancing will not make the most of it? You will have to go away and hide."

"No, she will not have to do that," Michael interrupted. "Because it is my intention to ask Miss Newton to become my wife!"

For one blissful moment Bettina heard only his beautiful words before reality rushed in and made her burst out,

"Oh, no, no, no!"

To marry the man she loved, only because he had been forced into it by duty?

It was unthinkable.

It would break her heart to refuse him, but she would

live broken-hearted all her days rather than destroy his life with a forced marriage.

Michael took her hands between his. He was very pale.

"My dear, your father is correct. I had no right to embroil you in this tangle just to save myself. It was selfish and thoughtless, for I never looked ahead to the harm that I might be doing you. But I certainly should have done."

"It does not matter," she cried desperately. "I will not marry you."

"And I say that you will," the Major declared in a commanding voice.

Bettina stared. Was this domineering man the gentle, loving father she had always known?

Had he too become infected with the desire to see his daughter marry a title?

"And I say that I will not," Bettina repeated.

She could hardly bear to look at Michael. What must he think of her?

Then she saw that he was looking at her with a half smile on his face that managed to be both kind and sad at the same time.

Gently he took her hands in his.

"The thought of marrying me is such a terrible prospect, isn't it?" he asked. "I do not blame you for not wanting to, but – " he seemed to have some difficulty finding the words, "do you not think you might bring yourself to reconsider?"

Suddenly she wanted to weep. There was an ache in her throat and she could not speak, only shake her head.

She tried to withdraw her hands, but he would not release them.

"Think about it," he begged. "Surely there is no –

other impediment to prevent us marrying?"

For the moment she did not understand him. Then she remembered.

"I regret to tell you, sir, that the 'other impediment' is *absolute.*"

"Then is it not time you told your father about him?"

"Told me what?" the Major asked sharply.

"Be brave, Bettina," Michael urged her. "Tell him everything."

"I will not," she said stubbornly. "This does not concern you, sir."

"But it concerns your father. He will want to know why you refuse me."

"I refuse you because I will not marry any man by these methods. The ordeal you dreaded most was to be forced into marriage."

"To Alice, not to you. And nobody can force me to do what I do not want to."

It was so tempting to believe him. There was a disturbing light in his eyes. She had dreamed of Michael looking at her like this.

But not in these circumstances.

"Nobody can force me, either," she declared, trying to sound decided. "I will not marry you, my Lord."

"Have you taken leave of your senses?" the Major demanded.

"Do not berate your daughter, sir," Michael said. "She cannot marry me because – "

"My Lord," Bettina called frantically.

"Because her heart is given to another."

The Major stared.

"Eh? What?"

"She has contracted an engagement that she fears would not meet with your approval and she is resolved to be true to her love."

"Stuff and nonsense!" the Major declared. "Bettina does not know any young men except Melroy Turvish in the lawyer's office and I would not stand in their way."

"You always said he was an idiot," Bettina protested.

"He *is* an idiot, but he is a respectable idiot, and if you had asked my approval, I would have said yes. Is it him?"

"No," she said wildly. "No, it isn't him."

She swung round on Michael.

"I wish I had never met you! I wish none of this had ever happened!"

She turned and raced away, out of the room, down the corridor, into the conservatory and out of doors, through the gardens and down to the river.

There she leaned against a tree trunk and burst into tears, wishing she could die of shame.

Her father was right. She would be ruined if she did not marry Michael, but after this episode, nothing would ever persuade her to marry him. She would rather live and die an old maid.

And that was exactly what would happen she realised.

But anything was better than living with a man she loved, knowing that he did not love her, seeing reproach in his eyes. Or, if not seeing it, imagining it.

At last she calmed herself. She must disappear from the village as soon as possible and never, never see Michael again.

She stepped away from the tree. It was time to start her new life, the hard bleak life that stretched ahead of her.

A life without him.

Drying her eyes as she ran, she missed her footing and stumbled against something warm and broad.

"You?"

"You didn't hear me approach," Michael said, holding onto her. "And I am glad that you didn't, otherwise you might have run away again. As it is," his arms tightened, "I have caught you and I will not let you go."

"Well, you must," Bettina replied, although she was not struggling.

"It was almost in this very spot that we first met, do you remember?"

"Yes I do and you behaved shockingly."

"True. And I am going to behave shockingly again."

The next moment his lips came down on hers. He pulled her closer and closer to him.

He had kissed her twice before, but this kiss was longer and sweeter.

To Michael it was as if he had suddenly swept her up into the sky and they were touching the stars.

Closer and still closer he drew her to him.

Bettina knew that she should be strong, but somehow she could find no strength to do anything except what he wanted.

Something strange and wonderful was happening to her, something that had never happened before.

To Michael it was what he had always longed for, but had never found until this moment.

At last he drew back and looked at her fondly.

"Please will you tell me the truth. Are you really engaged?"

She shook her head.

"I said it in anger."

"I hoped it was only that," he said. "I have been praying for a long time that there was no other man. And now there is no barrier to our marriage."

"Except that you do not want to marry me," she cried.

"Are you going to be that kind of wife, the kind who thinks she knows what I want better than I do?"

"I am not going to be your wife at all."

"Why? Because you do not love me? Your father thinks you do."

"I – you have talked this over with my father?"

"That is considered normal when a man wishes to marry a woman. I told him that I was in love with you and he said he was sure you felt the same. In fact, he has been convinced of it for some time. That is why he performed his imitation of a heavy-handed Papa. It was his way of playing Cupid!"

So her father had not changed after all, Bettina thought joyfully. He had divined her feelings and striven, as a loving father, to give her what she most desired.

"But I shall not believe it," Michael said, "until you tell me that you love me as much as I love you."

"You – love me?" she breathed.

"I love you as I never knew it was possible to love any woman. I believe my love for you started the day we met on this river bank, but it took me a while to see it."

Bettina made a sound and hid her face against his neck.

Michael's arms held her closer still.

"You are mine and I am yours completely. You must marry me. I cannot live without you."

He waited anxiously for her answer.

Then Bettina said in a whisper he could hardly hear,

"I love you, I love you, but how has this happened?"

"Because we were meant for each other," he said. "I have been searching for you all my life."

"I thought I was only useful to you," she answered, "to rid you of Alice."

"I think the truth is the other way round. Alice was really my excuse to become closer to you. I love you as I have never loved anyone in my life. The sooner we are married the sooner we can be together for always. I swear before God that I will make you happy."

His voice seemed to express even better than his words what he was feeling.

Bettina could only murmur,

"I love you. Oh, how I love you or I would never feel like this."

Michael kissed her. Then he said,

"Promise that you will marry me."

"I promise."

"We will be married quietly. Just your father, Win and Katherine and a few of the villagers. And, considering the circumstances, perhaps it had better be as soon as possible."

"You mean, considering that we are supposed to be already married?" she asked demurely but with a twinkle in her eye.

"That and the fact that we may not be safe until our wedding *has* taken place," he agreed. "I will not risk anything coming between us, my darling. Now that I have found you, I am going to keep you forever. I want you all to myself."

"And I want to be yours and nobody but yours," she sighed.

He smiled.

"Together we will make the castle and the garden so wonderful with our love," he promised.

"Only you could say something like that. I love you, I do love you. I have loved you since I first saw you, but I never thought I would ever belong to you."

"Do you think I would let anyone else have you?" Michael asked. "You are different from any woman I have known before. Now that we have found each other we will never be lonely or unhappy again."

"I will make you happy," Bettina vowed.

His arms wound about her again for the first kiss of their new avowed love. Bettina returned his kisses with all her heart and soul.

"Let us return now and ask the Vicar to marry us as soon as possible," he said at last, a little unsteadily.

"And as we go, beloved, sing to me again, the song you were singing on the day we met. Not the last part, for I will *never* leave you alone, but the beginning, which is about us and our love. *For we shall surely never be parted again*."

They walked away together, towards the glory of their future. Held in the circle of his arm, her head resting on his shoulder, Bettina began to sing.

Her sweet pure voice rang across the river and through the woods, echoing their song of true love.

"Where the sweet river wanders,

My love and I walked,

He smiled and said 'Dearest,

Come talk with me, talk.

Let's speak of the future

That shines bright before us,

And never, never be parted again'."

154